SNEAKERS IN THE WATER

NITA FARRIS

Copyright © Juanita Farris M&T Publishing 2017
Cover Illustration © Juanita Farris
ISBN 978-0-9991840-0-4
This title is also available in eBook

For Mason and Thyler.

The boy who changed my heart and the boy who changed my life.

SNEAKERS
IN THE
WATER

Chapter One

Claire
June 2015

It was the loneliest feeling on the planet, being alone while being surrounded by people you loved. I had received the best news of my entire life and every bit of me wanted to jump up and down. I wanted to scream and cry of happiness. To take a photo so I could remember this moment in its entirety.

Still, I was alone.

I was driving home from dinner with my mom and sister, my sister who had accomplished something she had never dreamed of. My news didn't even matter when eclipsed by the intensity of the two of them, supporting each other and filling the inside of my sisters Subaru with laughter that was almost contagious.

"Claire, please cheer up!" Terry shouted from the front seat.

I rolled my eyes and crossed my arms like a sullen child.

"No. I am so tired of feeling like an outsider in this family."

My mom, Marlo, sighed.

"What? Does that offend you?" I snapped. She turned to look at me, my own green eyes reflecting back to me.

"You're as far away as you want to be, Claire. It's time you realize that."

I looked down, my face burning with shame. Terry, ever the peacekeeper, looked into the rearview mirror to give me a sympathetic smile.

"Okay, put away the boxing gloves. We are celebrating."

My mom turned back around and patted Terry's hand as she rested it on the center console. I hated myself a little, wanting to steal a bit of my sister's thunder. But I couldn't help it.

"I know what we need!" Terry said, grinning and popping a CD into her stereo.

A poppy country song started playing softly, and she turned it up, wiggling her eyebrows at me in the rearview mirror. I looked down and forced away the grin that was tugging at my lips.

My freshman year of college I had gotten my hands on a fake ID and Terry found it in my wallet. I thought for sure she was going to confiscate it and tell our dad.

Instead, I got a lecture on how bars were more about the experience than drinking. She told me that if I ever got blackout drunk before my 21st birthday, she would write letters to every bar near my campus with a photo attached. She would make sure that I never got into another bar again.

Then, she took me to a karaoke bar for happy hour and bought me my first beer. It was one of the best nights I had ever shared with my sister. I sipped on a warm Budweiser, cringing every time but pretending to enjoy it and we decided to take the stage for the first time together.

Terry picked out a country anthem and started singing with such confidence that I envied her so much. I started off whispering under her alto voice, but little by little her enthusiasm was infectious and made me brave. Soon enough I was belting it out along with her. We were swaying our hips and making our voices way twangier than they needed to be.

It was the best.

At the next red stop light, Terry turned around and caught my eye.

"Let's go, girls," she said, smiling.

I took a deep breath, giving into her and her endless heart. Loving her for her success and for her wanting me to be a part of it. I rolled my eyes and sang the next line in my best Southern drawl.

"We're going out tonight. We're feeling alright."

The light turned green, Terry turned back around and began to turn onto the street where I lived with my dad. I closed my eyes, laughing and shaking my head. A squeal filled the car, drowning out Shania for a moment.

As I opened my eyes again, a red truck swerved into the intersection, bouncing like the suspension was made out of rubber

2

bands. Terry jumped and stepped on the gas, attempting to speed out of the way. I knew we were going to collide.

I slid down into my seat and reached out, trying to hold onto my mom and sister. And then we were upside down. I heard metal tearing and glass cut into my hands and face. My stomach rolled and my throat throbbed from the scream that tore through my chest. The car spun again and ended up on one side, my sister's seat pointed to the sky.

I blinked over and over, trying to make sense of what I was seeing. I was still inside, but what I saw around me didn't look like my sister's car anymore. Naked steel cut through the seats, and somehow, I could see the night sky through one of the windows.

I touched my forehead and blood stained my fingertips.

My sister.

"Terry?" I screamed, or rather, tried to. What came out of my mouth was more like a strangled whisper.

"Terry?" I tried to straighten in my seat so that I could see into the driver's seat.

There was so much glass, so much debris, and as much as I didn't want to see it, so much blood. I closed my eyes, wanting to give into the throbbing in my head and the fear that was suffocating me. I took a deep breath, trying to figure out what to do.

The radio struggled to turn back on, beeping static a few times before replaying the CD. It was a sick joke. My favorite memory of my sister, circling the CD player of her broken Subaru while she lay unconscious inches away from me.

I'd do anything for this not to be my last memory of her.

Terry
April 2015
Two Months Before

When I was in college earning my bachelor's degree in human services, one of my professors gave me a piece of advice that I never forgot.

She told me during a peer review that working with abuse victims would be the hardest thing I would ever do. I would need to be emotionally stable to do it every single day. She told me that she hung a beautiful poster of her favorite Monet painting on her ceiling, so it was the first thing and the last thing she saw at night. She began and ended every day with beauty because there was enough pain and ugliness in the world.

I never forgot that. When I started working as a counselor at Spokane Women's Center, the first thing I bought was a Princess Bride poster to tape above my bed. Not only is it a snapshot of my absolute favorite scene, Buttercup and Wesley holding each other in the gorgeous countryside after their adventure, but it brings to mind my very favorite memories.

Sitting on the couch with my sisters and mom, all sharing one blanket and a huge bowl of popcorn. Watching the Princess Bride and reciting Indigos speech by heart. It was a moment I could live in forever.

"Good morning," I whispered to my poster as I slid out of my dark green comforter and pushed my feet into unicorn slippers.

I adjusted the huge T-shirt I had slept in as I walked upstairs into the kitchen. My sisters and I had always slept on the lower floor. There were three rooms, a laundry room, and a living room we had used for sleepovers in middle school. The stairs led into the kitchen, which had a back door that my sister Claire snuck out of more than once.

My younger sister Macy was sitting at our small and scratched dining room table, eating half a bagel and updating her Facebook on my mom's tablet. Light the color of buttermilk streamed through the velvet curtains my mom had sewn while going through a crafty phase.

She ended up lugging her sewing machine back up to the attic, but we all loved the crooked curtains. The warm light gave the thin linoleum counters and peeling floor a more updated look than it deserved.

"Does the world need to be updated on your breakfast choice?" I asked, smiling and grabbing the Cocoa Puffs from the cupboard next to the fridge.

She rolled her eyes at me but grinned. My mom walked into the kitchen, already dressed in scrubs and holding a cup of coffee. I could hardly get over how beautiful she still was at 43. I always felt like I was looking into a mirror that predicted how I would look when I got older.

My mom and I both had unruly red hair that we wore close to our shoulders. We were curvy and short; I was three inches shorter than her and still held out hope that I would hit five feet somehow. We both had green eyes, but mine were soft where hers were searing. Macy did not have our red hair, but she had the dramatic flair that came with being a ginger.

"I know I'm dying to know. After Macy's fifth update of the day featuring her latest toenail polish, I was on the edge of my seat wondering what she would do next."

I giggled and grabbed the paperback I had started last night off the counter.

"I'd rather start my day with Edward."

"The pep rally is right after school, and then the football game lasts until around 11. Britney could drive me, and then you wouldn't even have to worry about it," Macy told my mom, pretending this was something she had already agreed to.

"Um, no. I will worry about it because Britney has only had her license for three months. And your curfew on weeknights is 10."

Macy's pink glossed lips thinned into a straight line, and she crossed her skinny arms across her chest.

5

"Am I supposed to leave the game before it's over? I have friends on the team; it's not fair to them or me."

My mom laughed and shook her head, "Being able to go the game is a privilege. You will be home at 10, and I will drive you, or you won't be going at all."

Macy stood and shook angrily into her backpack, "Fine. I'm going to miss the bus."

As she stomped out, my mom rolled her eyes, "Do you want me to drive you tonight? I will be home by 5:30 so you will need to be ready if you want to be there before kickoff."

"Yes, thank you," Macy dramatically sighed.

"Goodness," I said as the Macy less silence filled the kitchen.

"That girl will be the death of me. She has more drama inside of her than Days of Our Lives."

"It's a good thing you only have about fifteen years left until retirement. By then Macy will be long gone at college and giving her roommate's drama."

My mom gave me a brittle smile and squeezed my shoulders, "Yeah, but then I will miss it. This house is too quiet without my girls."

I kissed her cheek and watched her leave from the kitchen window as she headed for work. She was right; the house was quiet since we had grown up. I was happy to be able to move home and keep her company. I had been lonely a lot at university and coming back was like coming full circle for me.

I loved this house; I loved the memories that surrounded me in every room. I loved the couch downstairs with the nail polish stains on the arm and the incense that my mom lit for special occasions. I adored the paintings and family photos that cluttered every single wall.

I loved being able to watch my mother raise a teenager all alone and work her ass off at work. She inspired me every single day. After I finished my cereal, I rinsed the bowl, took a shower, and got ready for work myself.

I was a year into working at the center, but it still felt so new and exciting. Being able to make a difference in someone's life using my gift was so rewarding that it made the tough parts bearable.

I had been able to see the past through visions since I was young. This felt like the perfect way to share a part of myself that I usually had to keep hidden.

"Good morning, Lucy," I said to our receptionist as I passed her desk. She handed me a Starbucks cup, she always seemed to remember my current favorite, and answered the phone in front of her. I unlocked my office and opened my calendar for the day.

My first appointment was in five minutes, Sasha. Two months ago, she had left her abusive husband but having no money was making her transition impossible. I wasn't sure if many people understood that relationships could be financially abusive.

Not only did her husband control all of their money but he had convinced her that she would be unable to work. She seemed to believe him so far, and this step in her journey was significant to her recovery.

But even a new counselor like me knew that I couldn't make her want to move on or begin to support herself. It's an emotional step even more so than a financial decision.

A small knock jerked me from my thoughts, and I went to answer it. Sasha stood on the other side, wringing her hands until they were white.

"Hi, Sasha. Please come in."

As I offered her an armchair and I went to my desk for her case file before joining her. Immediately she broke down and admitted that she had moved back home with her husband. Money had gotten so low that she had to choose between shampoo and peanut butter. She hadn't eaten in two days when she ran into him at the recycling center trying to cash in bottles so that she could buy maxi pads.

He had taken her to lunch and begged her to take him back. She had agreed. Part of me wondered if he knew she would have to resort to the recycling center and staked it out to find her. It didn't feel impossible.

"Has he hit you since you have been home?" I asked, trying not to look terrified of the answer.

She shook her head furiously, "No. It's been perfect, like being newlyweds again. That's why I made my appointment today."

"You are going to continue coming to sessions? I think that's a fantastic idea, especially while both of you are recovering from your past altercations."

Sasha stared at the carpet under my desk, "No. I wanted to tell you goodbye. Things are going to be different. Jared and I both decided it was best if we recovered together in private."

"I would have to advise against that," I said, struggling to sound calm.

She met my eyes, tears in the rims.

"Goodbye, Terry. I have loved coming here and am so grateful for your support. But things are going to be different."

I watched her nod firmly like she was trying to convince the both of us. I leaned forward and touched her hand. My hand didn't even twitch as warmth ran up my arm, I closed my eyes for half a second and received a lifetime of emptiness.

Sasha is kneeling on a kitchen floor, cleaning up broken dishes still covered in food. She had somehow ruined dinner, though I didn't think putting gravy on the meatloaf instead of mashed potatoes was so catastrophic. It certainly didn't warrant the fresh cigarette burns she was hiding under the quarter sleeve of her light blue T-shirt.

I opened my eyes and gave her a sad smile, running my hand up her arm until my fingers brushed the burns still healing under her sleeve. Her eyes widened, but she didn't lose her poker face.

"I pray that things are different from now on. I will always be here if you need to talk."

She crossed her arms then rushed out of the room. I sighed, settling back into my seat. Why had I said that I would pray? I hadn't prayed since I was 14 and my dad told me that Jesus didn't give people psychic gifts. He stated that the only reason I could see the past was that I must be committing a sin, and this was my punishment.

8

It was only one of the million reasons there wasn't a photo of my dad here, where I needed to be emotionally sound. My mom was convinced that our gifts were from God, that something this good had to be divine.

But I wasn't always sure. How could God stand by and watch a husband burn curse words into his wife's back and then allow her to forgive him? What kind of gift would a God like that give?

*

"It hasn't been physical in a while, but I still feel myself walking on eggshells. I am constantly terrified no matter how he is acting. When will that feeling go away?" Gina asked.

Today was our fourth meeting, and she seemed stuck in the same spot. She was still with her abusive fiancé, Lucas, making excuses for him and believing that she was the problem.

"Well, like I said last time, it's his actions that are creating this toxic cycle. As long as he refuses to acknowledge the past abuse you two will never be able to start over. It will continue to cycle. Abuse, an apology, and the calm before the inevitable storm."

Gina took a deep breath and leaned back in her chair, "I wish I could fix it. I want our relationship back to what it was. He loved me once. I think maybe that I have changed. Became harder to love. Maybe I expect too much out of him. My mom, she always told me that love was supposed to be easy. Not like you didn't have to work on it, but the loving another person part."

"I don't know about easy, but you should never have to worry about your partner's intentions. It does take two to make it work."

She hugged herself and was still nervously biting her lip, leaving a red ring around one edge. She looked at her cell phone and stood up.

"I guess my hour is over. I will see you in the next couple weeks?" I stood as well, leaning forward to shake her hand.

As our skin touched, I dropped to my knees. Snapshots tore through my head. Tile, black, white, and blue. A hospital bed with baby blue sheets and older woman lying under them. Her eyelids flutter open, and she sighs faintly. As she tries to speak a pillow covers her face, blurry hands hold it down as she struggles, her nails trying to tear at the arms.

I recoil against her flailing, feeling her breath tighten, tighten, until there is nothing left to draw into her lungs. It's almost a relief when her breathing stops, and her heart slowly lies still.

"Terry?! Terry!"

I feel hands grip my shoulder and shake me slightly. I blink and focus on Gina's face and grasp her arm, expecting another piece of the vision to course through me. But all I receive is her undiluted fear and panic.

It slips into my veins, making me nauseous and faint.

"Terry, do you need me to get some help?"

I pull myself into a chair and put my head between my knees, breathing deeply as I began to feel more stable in my world. I looked up slowly; Gina was still kneeling on the ground, staring at me with her mouth gaping.

"I am so sorry, Gina. I have low blood sugar and got super dizzy all of a sudden," I told her, a lie I had used a lot during college when I would become overwhelmed unexpectedly.

"It's okay. Are you sure you are alright?" she said, standing and brushing off her jeans.

I nodded, "Of course. I just need to eat."

Slowly I stood with her and walked her out to our lobby where we made her next appointment. After she left, I turned to Lucy, beginning to feel sweaty and faint once again.

"I think I am coming down with something. I am going to take the rest of the day off. Please apologize to my last two appointments for me."

She tried to recover but couldn't hide the surprise on her face. I never called in sick and I certainly never left in the middle of the day.

Then again, I had never gotten a vision that physical before.

I had touched Gina, but Gina wasn't in the vision. This look into the past was different, it was high definition, and I knew it was more important than any image I had ever had. It didn't feel like a random moment my psyche grabbed onto. This was meant for me.

I grabbed my purse and headed to my car quickly. As I reached my driver's door, I was overcome with residual panic and leaned over to vomit.

I wiped my mouth, sat down in my car and wrote down as much as I could about my flash. I closed my eyes, trying to focus on my intuition. The tile, the hospital room, the elderly lady, the fear. The tile, I had seen that flooring many times before.

The black, white, and blue squares pieced together were exactly like the floor in the patient rooms at my mom's work.

I sent her a message that I was on my way over with a family emergency and took a swig of water, trying to erase the taste of death that was still lingering on the back of my teeth.

*

"Mom, I'm telling you this was different. Closer to the present than anything I have ever seen," I said, trying to stay calm.

It had been a week since I had come to my mom with my unsettling vision. She had been dealing with a difficult patient that day and listened to me, but she was quick to dismiss that it had anything to do with Olive Grove.

"Can you usually tell the actual day that the flashbacks come from? Maybe your gift is evolving," my mother said.

"Kind of not the point."

She sighed.

"Okay. I accept that this felt huge to you. But how do you know it's connected to Olive Grove?"

"As I told you, I recognized the tile. It was an older lady in a hospital bed."

"But how many nursing homes have that kind of tile?"

I leaned forward to force her to make eye contact with me. I never challenged my mom; she knew I was serious.

"Okay, how about this. The vision came to me. A vision of an older lady being smothered to death in a nursing home with tile exactly like Olive Groves. It's important because I have never gotten a vision since beginning working at the shelter that didn't matter. We are supposed to do something about this."

"But, you see the past; doesn't that mean that it has already happened. That whoever the vision showed you is already gone?"

My mouth trembled, and I suddenly felt the need to cry. The thought hadn't even crossed my mind. I closed my eyes to picture the flash again. It was wobbly like I saw the photograph through muddy water.

"I don't think it has happened yet? Or the ending was different," I whispered.

My mom put her hands over mine.

"You saw the future?"

I opened my eyes and looked at her, bewildered.

"I'm not sure. But I do know that whoever that lady is, her soul is still here. Do you want to be responsible for someone that you have watched over dying alone and terrified? She was frail, but she fought right up until her last breath. I could feel her lungs screaming for air. Unless we find her and help her, she is going to die a horrible lonely death."

My mom sat back in her chair; her eyes shimmery with tears.

"Okay. I will help you. Shadow me for a day, meet my patients and feel for whatever signs there might be. But if you don't feel anything, we move to another nursing home and search from there."

I took a relieved breath, glad to be taking some action finally. I had been re-living the vision in my dreams for the last couple of weeks. They didn't feel like dreams though; I was trapped in the senior woman's body. I knew I was going to be attacked and fought back with everything I had. I always woke up choking for air and believing I had suffocated along with her.

Chapter Two

Claire
June 2015

As I hung in the air, the sounds around us seemed to fade one by one. The dog barking on the next block deadened to a wheeze. The alarms we somehow set off stopped in mid-beep.

A car idled next to us. I heard a car door slam and footsteps made their way to where I was hanging.

"Hello?" I choked out.

The footsteps faded, and the car sped away. Then almost silence. Another sound was growing. A clawing against the cement. I could see Terry's hand dangling, but my mom must have been thrown out of the car. Was that her trying to get help?

"Mom?" I said quietly, the only volume I could muster.

The sound paused for a second before quickening. I needed to help her.

"Oof."

All the air escaped from my chest as I finally slid onto the street. The car wasn't fully upside down. Instead, it was lying on one side sloppily.

My mom's seat seemed to blend into the asphalt of the street. I fumbled with her seat belt, incredibly thankful that it clicked open quickly.

Goosebumps broke out on my arm. My mom was still in her seat. What the hell was that noise? We were in the middle of town; it was impossible that animals would have been prowling.

My mom fell limply into my arms, and I did my best to pull her out of the car without dragging her now bare feet across the street. I wanted to call for help but my phone was in my purse and I couldn't see it anywhere. I searched for my moms instead.

As I found her phone wedged in her front pants pocket, I held my breath. Hoping with all my might that it would still work. I began

13

to sob as I tried to power it up and realized the screen was smashed.

I put my mom's head in my lap and leaned down to try to hear her breath. My ears were ringing; a man came running out of his house down the block.

He started screaming at me, waving a phone around and gesturing for me to get away from the car. All I could hear was ringing; I strained to hear her breath, even just a whisper. The man stood where he was, talking into his phone and gesturing wildly to the otherwise empty street.

I closed my eyes to block him out as the ringing in my ears began to subside. I shook my head, refusing to accept the fact that my mom's breath wasn't coming. I put my hand on her chest, no rising. No falling. I thought I felt an irregular heartbeat, but that could have been my own.

I had begun to feel breath against the back of my neck that couldn't belong to my mother or sister. Something told me to keep my eyes shut, to keep my hand on my mom's chest, to will her heart to keep pounding until the paramedics arrived and could save us both.

Terry

April 2015

"This is the weirdest Easter gathering I have ever been to," CJ said.

He was helping me mix the potato salad by trying to steal bites with the ladle.

"Is it that bad?" I asked quietly, looking out the kitchen door to make sure my mom wasn't in the dining room and able to hear us.

"It's your mom, your sister, your sister's girlfriend, and us. Where's Claire?" he asked, shaking his head.

"Shhh!" I peeked out the kitchen door, looking for everyone else.

Macy, Britney, and Mom were in the middle of playing Taboo. I took my place back at the counter with CJ.

"Claire decided that she was going to stay at her dorm for Easter. She said she needed to study."

"It's the last big holiday before graduation. When was the last time she was home?"

I sighed.

"Christmas. Where she told Mom that my dad's house was her home. It was awful. She claimed she wasn't trying to start a fight, but it made our mom cry."

"What brought that up?"

"Mom told her that when she graduated, she could move back in with us. That she had been gone long enough."

CJ shook his head again.

"That's a sore subject. Why would either one of them go there?"

I shrugged.

"Who knows. It's not a holiday unless someone is locking themselves in the bathroom crying. We drag up painful memories instead of playing Parcheesi."

He pulled himself up onto the counter to see my face as I stirred the salad.

15

"Not this year, okay? Britney and I are here; it's not going to be like last year."

I shook my head.

"Do you remember elementary school when your mom and dad were still married, and they would put on massive egg hunts in your backyard? Inside were strips of paper that fit together to tell the story of Jesus's life," CJ said, smiling.

"Yeah, I do. I don't miss pretending to believe in God, but I do miss it feeling like an actual family holiday. Know what I mean?"

"I do. But that doesn't mean we can't make new memories."

I carried the potato salad out to the dining room and put it next to the ham CJ had made. I straightened the plates and place settings.

"It's hard to imagine sometimes. A future life with a husband that accepts our gifts and doesn't feel like I will be passing down the genetic equivalent of hell in a bottle."

He put his arm around me.

"Who needs a husband? Your best friend accepts and loves you just the way you are."

I looked up at him.

"Visions included?"

"Shortcake, I couldn't care less. I would love you even if you had x-ray vision and flew."

He smiled broadly but moved to the other side of the table, looking down at the plates and straightening the tablecloth.

"But?" I asked, knowing he was holding back.

"This last one, with that Gina girl? It sounded intense. Sometimes I worry that it's getting too powerful and that your body won't be able to handle it," he said, locking eyes with me, sounding ashamed of being scared.

I crossed the room to hug him.

"I will be okay. I promise."

He turned to look me in the eyes, squeezing me back.

"Okay, okay. Break it up," Macy said, coming in holding hands with Britney. I laughed and rolled my eyes, "Macy, knock it off."

Britney looked at Macy with confused eyes. Macy beamed at her, knowing how strange today must already be for her but proud of us regardless.

"Terry and CJ are friends, always have been. But I believe they are secretly in love. I also think they won't figure it out until they are in their 40s and are wondering why they never married."

CJ and I held each other's eyes with a grin. I had struggled with my feelings for CJ for what felt like my whole life. But most of the time I was peaceful, every part of my heart knew that he wasn't meant to be mine.

We took our seats and had a moment of silence in case anyone wanted to pray, CJ always did.

"Speaking of CJ, isn't it time you started thinking about settling down?" mom said, giving him a stern look as she passed him the rolls.

"No way, and miss out on all that online dating has to offer?"

"You do that?!"

I laughed, "Tell her about your date on Thursday."

He visibly brightened.

"I have been talking to this girl named Shayla for a couple of months. She kept asking me the craziest questions like she was testing me for something. I ended up getting her to agree to hang out, but she would only see me during the day. I was for sure she thought I was a serial killer and I thought maybe I could woo her over coffee."

My mom nodded, looking horrified at the thought of meeting with a stranger.

"She insisted on picking me up, and instead of Starbucks, she took me to a laundry mat. She pulled all these bags of clothes out of her trunk and told me that she was never going to be a housewife to someone who didn't appreciate it. She said that if I were going to be her husband, I would have to pull my weight. I had to prove I knew how to wash laundry."

"She wanted you to... Wash her laundry? That's it?"

He winked, making everyone laugh. I loved how he drew the story out.

"And?" I said, pushing him to the end of the story.

"So, I agreed, under one condition. I wanted her to feed me afterward because I was never going to cater to someone who didn't appreciate it. That if we were splitting future chores, then she had to prove that she could cook."

My mom choked on her lemonade, "Tell me she didn't go for that."

CJ grinned smugly, "I did her laundry, perfectly I might add. Folding included. Then she took me home where she made me carne asada, tortillas, and salsa. Then we made out for three hours."

Macy's eyes widened, and she laughed.

"That's bizarre. Did you delete her immediately?"

"Um no. She made amazing tortillas. I have another date with her on Saturday. We are supposed to go to a movie, and then I am making dinner for her at my apartment."

Everyone stared at him, unsure whether or not to take him seriously.

"You know, future chore-splitting and all. She cooked last time, so it's CJ's turn. But you can bet your ass she is going to have to wash the dishes," I said, grinning at him.

*

"Dad?" I said, unlocking my dad's back door when no one answered the front door.

The house was dark, but I could hear and see the TV from the living room. I relocked the back door and put the lasagna I had brought over in the fridge. Walking through my dad's apartment always filled me with a sense of pity.

It felt like someone else had picked out the furniture, someone who also decorated office buildings to make them as impersonal as possible. Gray chairs and couches, chrome appliances, walls and counters divulge of any mementos or photos.

I was always left with the idea that my dad could up and leave whenever he wanted. There would be nothing here that would miss him. The rooms would go on without him.

"Dad?" I called again, coming into the living room.

He was asleep in front of the TV, the remote still in his hand and his chin resting on his chest as he stretched out in his recliner. I quietly crossed the room and took the remote from his hand, intending to turn off the TV for him.

hand froze as I saw what was playing on the screen.

My mom wiped tears from her eyes as she held my dad's hand in front of a justice of the peace. Their wedding video. They had gotten eloped, a package that included a video, an 8x10 photo, and a marriage certificate.

This video used to make me sad. I wondered if my mom wished that she had been able to have a huge wedding with a Vera Wang dress. But I guess that wouldn't have fit my dad, who was a natural loner.

It was still the week of Easter, and he made no plans. His parents still lived in Florida, but he chose to be alone so often. I couldn't figure out why he would watch something like this by himself, did he want to be depressed?

I glanced at him, seeing tears drying on his cheeks. My heart lurched. I was so mad at my dad most of the time, but I knew the divorce wasn't fully his fault. He had grown up religious, anything supernatural would have been deemed satanic immediately.

So, when he met my mom, he was in love before he found out about her psychic gift. Maybe he thought she wasn't serious, that it was a phase she would outgrow.

He wanted her to be normal. He wanted them to raise their daughters in the church and teach them the "right way."

My dad missed her, so much that even after fifteen years he was still watching videos of a time when he thought he had found his soul mate. Mom thought she had as well.

Maybe I thought of the divorce differently because I had been the one to watch my mom nurse a broken heart. My sisters had been protected from that. The early days after my dad left were anything but easy.

I don't think Claire and Macy understood what was going on. They kept asking me when he was coming home. My mom kind of went into herself for that first week.

She stopped cleaning the house, she stopped cooking, and she stopped living. I ended up being the one that told the girls that this was permanent. They didn't react right away; it was over Macy's head altogether.

Later on, that Claire was helping me fold laundry and pulled one of our dad's T-shirts out of the basket.

"Where do I put this?" she asked, her face twisted in pain.

I took a deep breath.

"I don't know. Maybe we should put it in a bag? For him to take?"

"We are packing for him?" Claire asked, tears squeezing out of her beautiful green eyes.

I had always been jealous that she was the only one that shared mom's exact shade of green. Mine matched Dad's, the person who was making Claire cry right now.

I couldn't believe he had left pieces of his life behind for us to find. For us to have to clean up. I took Claire into my arms and let her cry herself out. Then I sent her to play and finished the laundry myself.

That night I brought a bowl of soup to my mom and saw that the three previous plates I had brought her were sitting on her dresser untouched. I was filled with anger and felt so helpless.

"Mom, you should know... if you don't eat, I am not going to either."

She looked at me with dead eyes then rolled over. I took the plates back to the kitchen then threw them into the trash along with my dinner.

Three days later she finally emerged from her bedroom, her hair was a greasy mess, and her nails were bitten to bleeding. Our house was cleaned as much I was capable of as a child, but it was clear that every room had been left to neglect, as the kids that occupied them.

Claire and Macy were sitting at the table eating peanut butter sandwiches, and I was catching up on homework.

"Where's your sandwich?" Mom asked me, sitting at the table.

"I wasn't kidding," I told her, not even looking up from my science workbook.

Her face finally broke into a startled grimace.

"Terry, that was three days ago."

I shrugged; my stomach seemed to grumble on cue. Her eyes shone with tears, but she stood up and went over to the cupboard. She got out bread, cheese, and butter and made us both huge grilled cheese sandwiches.

She put mine down in front of me as Claire and Macy left to play Barbie's. I locked eyes with her, waiting until she took the first bite before I even touched mine. She ate hers then broke down into sobs.

Apologizing. Promising to pull herself back together. I got up and wrapped her in my arms. She missed Dad more than anything, but she couldn't change who she was.

He wanted the impossible. Mom wasn't "normal." She could never be who he or Claire wanted her to be. She wasn't perfect, but she was extraordinary. I wished with all my heart he would see that someday and love all of us the way that we were.

I turned off the TV, leaving those memories behind. I kissed my dad on his still damp cheek, wrote him a note to tell him I had left dinner for him, and locked the door behind me. Locking those memories behind me.

*

The white, black and blue tiles flashed beneath my feet as I followed my mom to the nurse's station. She still didn't want me to be here, and I could feel her doubt flowing through her in waves. I wanted to help, but all she could see was the possibility of people she worked so hard to protect being exploited.

21

I took a deep breath, looking around as my mom checked in. I thought I would feel an explosion of sensation, a voice pulling me towards a particular room perhaps.

Instead, I was soaked with tangible sadness I walked around Olive Grove with my mother. I shadowed her and helped out when she needed me. I watched her braid patient's hair and smiled as she helped them brush their teeth and fed them patiently.

She made her patients' lives bright, but this place was still not home. Pain saturated this building right down the concrete foundation.

"Anything?" my mom asked me quietly as she filled outpatient logs and set up a cart to administer medication.

I shook my head and stared down at my hands fretfully.

"Maybe I made a mistake?"

My mom bit her lip; she didn't want me to be wrong if it meant someone died before their time. But she also didn't expect me to be right.

"How is it usually for you? When you see someone's destiny, and it's violent?" I asked.

My mom rocked on her heels.

"I haven't seen a violent end in a long time."

"No?" I asked, confused.

She shook her head, "I think... The last one I saw was when you were in middle school. I was in the grocery store and touched hands with our cashier while buying milk. I saw that she was going to have a car accident in two weeks. I asked her if she drove and she said no, smiling. I found out from the obituary two weeks later that she had just turned sixteen and had been hit while learning to drive. Her older brother had been killed as well. I saw the whole thing, right down to the paramedics trying to perform CPR on her."

I touched her arm.

"I'm sorry, Mom."

"That's why this is also my safe place. These deaths have meaning because they are supposed to happen when they do. It doesn't always feel fair or seem like everyone gets as much time as they want. But, there's a simplicity in dying from old age that makes

22

me feel like my gift is being put to good use. I can be their last reason to smile. Violence isn't supposed to happen here, and if I see it happen, I can prevent it."

I fidgeted, realizing why it was so hard for my mom to understand my reasons for coming today. In my mom's world, my vision taking place here was impossible. She made sure of that.

I followed her through the rooms, giving afternoon medication and catching up with her patients after a weekend off.

"Hi, Cathy," my mom said quietly, coming into a room after knocking solidly.

A woman looked up at us, startled from a nap.

"Good afternoon, dear. It's time for your medication," my mom said softly.

My mom gave her a moment to wake up by getting her a glass of water and sitting on her bed. Cathy jerked her head and held out her hands.

Without even having to ask I could see the signs of Alzheimer's. Notes with her name written on it, the name of the home, a big calendar with the date and year prominently stated.

I meandered around the room.

"Marlo?" Cathy asked, blushing as she said it.

"That's right," my mom said, nodding with encouragement in her eyes.

Cathy's eyes slid to me, and I could tell she was wondering if I was another test question, she was bound to get wrong.

I held out my hand.

"I'm Terry, Marlo's daughter. I'm shadowing my mom for a day."

She let out a breath, relieved that I was a new face. She leaned forward to take my hand. In that brief shake, a red-hot jolt ran up my arm. I was able to keep myself from clamping down on her fingers but wasn't able to keep from closing my eyes as the same snapshot of suffocation gripped my body.

I took a labored deep breath and stepped back from her, gently dropping her hand.

Cathy didn't notice my behavior, but my mom straightened with a pained look as she watched me. As she finished up, I excused myself and went to the nurse station bathroom to throw up.

The same panic filled my stomach and decay crept up my throat. The smell of antiseptic made it hard to take a rejuvenating breath.

My mom knocked on the door, and I gingerly opened it as I washed the taste out of my mouth.

"Cathy?" she asked, almost a whisper.

I took a deep reviving breath.

"I'm positive. The hands that fought off the attacker wore a bracelet with a sparrow charm. It's the same bracelet Cathy was wearing today. I could see her room in the background; it's the same bed. The same everything."

Except it wasn't. Something was different that I couldn't put my finger on. But it was Cathy fighting for her life. That much I was sure of.

My mom sank into a seat with a look of complete defeat on her face.

"Mom, you can't blame yourself."

"But I can Terry," she snapped.

I stepped back, stung.

She reached for my hand, apologizing with her eyes.

"I see the future Terry, I always have. My gift has never withheld from me. Why now? If you hadn't met her today, would we know what her future held for her?"

"I don't know. But I did see it, and you brought me here. Maybe we are getting all the pieces we need; we only need to put them together."

"What did you say your patient's name was?" my mom asked, opening the folder.

"Gina, why?"

She pointed to a form in front of her. I leaned forward, shocked as I read the line my mom pointed to with her pen. Gina Carlton, emergency contact. She was Cathy's daughter.

"So, we have the connection. We are supposed to help Gina save her mom."

My mom slowly tilted her head forward, "I think so."

I sat next to her, "How?"

"You know, I wonder if you actually saw something in the future," my mom said thoughtfully.

I took a sharp intake of breath, hurt. Seeing my reaction, my mom shook her head.

"No, sweetheart. That's not what I mean. Cathy has been here for two years. She was brought in after the ambulance was called to her home, where they thought she had a stroke."

"Do you not think it was? A stroke I mean?"

"I think it was a stroke. Put into motion by someone trying to end her life by force."

Chills broke out on my arm. Then why the vision? Why bring me here over something that happened years ago? My mom seemed to read my mind and leaned forward and took my hand.

"Because it was something I couldn't see, but something you could. Maybe the person who tried to hurt her two years ago has decided to finish the job."

I was suddenly tearful as I accepted the enormity of the situation. Getting the initial vision had almost been exciting. But now, someone could die because the system would never take us seriously.

I have always been unsure of why God would give us gifts that made us so miserable sometimes. But this was something else. Did he have the balls to dangle a death over us and make us believe we could prevent if we couldn't?

Would he show us this only to have us watch this life slip through our hands regardless of how hard we fought to keep Cathy safe?

Chapter Three

Claire
June 2015

The breath came hot and fast on my neck as I caressed my mom's cheek. I knew she was unconscious and possibly slipping away.

Still, I wasn't moved by any urgency.

I felt like I was watching it from inside someone else's body. I adjusted my legs on the cement, my eyes falling on black smudges underneath me.

Black handprints encircled the car. They were smudged in places like the hands had been dragging a body behind them. The handprints led over to where I was sitting. To behind me. Where the breath was consistently trained on my neck.

"Don't turn off the radio," Terry choked out from the other side of the car.

My breath caught in my throat as I realized that I had left her inside of the car that was still lying on its side. Gently I laid my mom's head on the asphalt.

As I got to my knees to stand up the breath on the back of my neck suddenly disappeared and left only freezing cold behind.

Terry hung upside down, her arms flailing as she grasped her seat belt.

"Let me help you."

She shook her head slowly.

"It's stuck."

I looked around and grabbed a piece of glass that had shattered from the now empty windshield.

"Let me try. Put your hands straight out to help brace your fall when it starts to loosen. We don't want you bumping your head."

We looked at each other for a moment, both accepting how silly that sounded.

I began sawing at the lap section of Terry's seat belt, the glass cutting into my hand and becoming slimy with blood. It broke off enough for me to rip it the rest of the way and I squatted so that Terry would slide into my lap.

"The radio," Terry said softly.

I settled on the ground with her.

"It's on, sweetheart. The radio is still on."

She shuddered.

"Don't let the music slip away. It's so quiet when I close my eyes."

Despite my pleading, her eyelids closed. I began to cry again. Don't let the music slip away. I brought my head close to her ear, rocking slightly.

"Men's shirt, short skirt, ooh ohh ohh," I sang softly to her.

I thought back to the karaoke bar and how my sister wasn't afraid to dance across the stage. It was that Terry I held in my arms instead of the broken Terry in front of me.

As the ambulance came around the corner, I closed my eyes, holding her tight before they pulled her away.

This was my punishment for holding them so far from my heart. I had kept my mom and sister at a distance my whole life, so now I was forced to watch them die by degrees.

Terry

April 2015

"You were right; you were always right. It's never going to stop," Gina told me.

She was gingerly touching the fresh bruise made up across her left cheekbone. I locked eyes with her, trying to stay focused. I was shocked when Gina came back into the office.

She had seemed so unsure about our counseling sessions when I had seen her last. I had never doubted that Lucas would continue to be abusive, but my vision left me feeling like I would never see her again.

As Gina recounted what she had been through I was burning to tell her about what I had seen and to ask her a million questions.

But a low warning resonated inside of me, telling me that it wasn't the right time and that I could mess up being able to help Cathy by letting Gina know.

"Are you fully moved out? You didn't leave anything that he can hold over your head and make you come back for?" I asked, crossing my legs and trying to take notes.

She shook her head.

"No. I mean technically it's my house, but I don't want it right now if it means seeing him. I am staying with a friend from high school that he has never met. I am terrified; I feel like I need to hide."

"Let yourself heal. We will deal with the legal repercussions as they come and when you are ready to handle them. But right now, all that matters is that you are safe."

But is Cathy? After penciling Gina in for an appointment in a week, I trudged home. Being in the same room with her and wanting to touch her was emotionally exhausting.

Usually, I refrained from forcing visions because I knew that it could cloud what I saw. I might see only half of the story or an

28

altered version of the events that the person constructed to protect themselves.

Until they are ready to be read, it's difficult to know what actually happened. What would I see with Gina the next time she opened up enough? Would it already be too late?

"Hey," I said to my mom.

I kissed her on the side of the head as I dropped my purse onto the kitchen table next to her and went to the fridge for a bottle of Pepsi.

"Hey," she said, turning to face me.

"Where's Mac?" I asked, unscrewing the lid and tossing it onto the counter.

"With Britney. They have a big test tomorrow and are supposed to be studying. So, they are probably at the school kissing with open textbooks on their lap. I'm sure they will do fine."

I smiled, but my mom didn't return it.

"What's up?" I asked.

She looked down at her hands.

"How was work?" my mom asked.

I sat down across from her, my stomach clenching in panic.

"I saw Gina again today. She has left Lucas and was really beat up. But I feel like you know that already. What happened?"

My mom looked up at the ceiling, her tell for trying to collect her thoughts.

"Remember when we talked about how the future could change and how emotional turmoil could solidify a decision?"

"Gina being beat changed something? For Cathy?"

"Only that now I can see her death."

My breath caught in my chest, fighting to be released. My mom looked defeated, and I realized she never wanted me to be right. I tried not to feel offended, but it was hard. I wanted to help Cathy just as much as she did.

"I was brushing Cathy's hair today and barely grazed her temple. It was so much that I collapsed. I have never experienced something that intense in my entire life."

I put a hand to my mouth, shivering.

29

"I saw everything. But from Cathy's perspective. The pillow, I felt her try to claw away. I felt the life ebb away from her until nothing was left and we were floating away."

I closed my hand over her cold palm. My nightmare came back into my mind, and I could still taste cotton on my tongue.

"But there was something more. Usually, when I have a vision, I know that it's right for them, there is no panic, there is peace, and the light is so close that it barely takes a breath to bring them to an end. This time, it was a darkness that was after Cathy. Her light was being snuffed out, and the edges of the action were being pushed back. It wasn't her time. A murder can be part of someone's destiny, but it is not part of Cathy's."

We looked at each other as the minutes ticked by on the huge gaudy clock hanging next to the fridge.

"What should we do?" my mother asked me.

It was the first time my mom had ever asked me that question, expected my lead. It frightened me more than anything.

"I wish I knew," I answered, fear filling my chest.

*

"Gina, it's me again. I wanted to see how you were doing and wanted to spend some time talking with you. Please call me back. You know the number."

Leaving the fifth message in one week was beginning to feel a little overboard, but I was getting worried. After leaving Lucas, Gina had come into the office twice a week. For the past week, I hadn't heard from her at all. I had this awful feeling that she had taken him back and he had really hurt her.

But I couldn't do more than reaching out, and I couldn't even really identify myself on the messages.

Sighing, I headed over to my filing cabinet to look at her file for the hundredth time. As I flipped through it, my stomach contracted at the sight of her hospital photographs from last year. Lucas had broken two of her ribs for trying a new hair dye. How controlling abusive husbands were never ceased to amaze me.

30

They not only wanted to be the boss when it came to who you spend time with and what you said but might even try to dictate what you wore when you were at home waiting to make them dinner. It was insanity.

I had Gina's home address memorized by now but knew I would get fired if I tried to stop by and she complained. But maybe my mom could try. Dialing the number from memory I got to my mom's work phone, knowing she was on lunch.

"Hello?"

"Hey, it's me. How's your day going?" She paused, taking a silent deep breath.

"It's okay. I forgot my lunch in the fridge at home, so I am cheating on my diet with some Mc Donald's."

I sat up, feeling the lie in her voice.

"I'm sorry. I could have brought you something."

"No, that's okay," she said, a little too quickly.

"Mom, what's wrong? You sound weird. What happened?"

She paused again, wanting to avoid the conversation.

"Mom."

"Okay, okay. We had a strange week with Cathy."

"Week? Why didn't you say something?" I asked, shutting Gina's file in worry.

"Because it's her family's business. I am not used to talking about patients with people who don't work here. It's HIPPA, you know that," she said, sounding frustrated.

I closed my eyes, feeling stung. I did know; I worked with HIPPA every single day. It was the red tape that bound my wrist together when I wanted to help a patient that didn't want any.

"I'm sorry. I'm trying to help."

"No, I'm sorry. This whole situation is starting to bug me. I can't do it on my own; it's not just helping someone into the next life. This is forcing something that should be natural."

I kept quiet, letting her collect herself.

"But... I am starting to see that we need to intervene even though I hate the idea. I got Gina's address from Cathy's medical

31

records. I need to speak to her, to warn her. It's the only way I know how to protect Cathy."

"I'm coming with you."

*

I knew Cathy's condition was going to have to suffer before my mom would get involved but being faced with the reality of it still broke my heart. My mom seemed to be absorbing some of her pain.

Cathy was beginning to have lucid moments where she became terrified, even violent. But she wouldn't let anyone call Gina. Cathy didn't want to be an even bigger burden to her.

She had started talking about being ready for death, so others didn't have to worry about her. Saying things like life would be better if she was gone so everyone could move on. My mom wanted to talk to Gina about Cathy's treatment and how to best help her.

If the family wasn't involved, it was a lot harder to help your patient. She let me come but only under the condition that I stay in the car. I wasn't a fan of the idea of being fired, so I agreed.

Gina's house was well-kept on the outside. It was light blue with navy trim and immaculate flower beds framed a walk-in porch. The driveway was empty, and I hope Lucas' truck wasn't waiting in the detached garage.

My mom had gone in only fifteen minutes earlier but was already leaving the house looking disheveled. I started the car and drove us home before beginning to ask any questions. Once home my mom collapsed into a kitchen chair and took a deep breath.

"Gina has some problems, is it only the guy?"

I shrugged, "She doesn't do drugs or abuse alcohol as far as I can tell. But she is having trouble fully shaking her fiancé. He has complete control over her life and puts her in the hospital about every six months. Why? Did you see more?"

My mom shrugged, "I guess I have never been confronted by someone who lived in that kind of fear constantly. I told her about

32

her mom, how terrified she has become. Gina seemed to fly into a panic when I told her that it was from experiencing lucid moments. She wanted to know exactly what her mom's words were, who she was afraid of. Honestly, it seemed like she was protecting someone. Do you think she knows that he hurt her and would go along with it if he tried again?"

I wrapped my arms around myself, sick at the idea, "I hope not... But on some level, it makes sense because the vision came from her. Maybe Cathy tried to stop the abuse? But why would he go after her again? She's already in a home."

My mom gave me a sad look, "Nursing homes like ours can be expensive. Does Gina work?"

"Part-time at a jewelry counter in the mall. Lucas doesn't want her out of the house a ton."

She flipped through the files, "Then he is probably paying for the care unless Gina stands to inherit a lot of money."

I sat back in my chair, disgusted, "She made you leave?"

"She was afraid he was going to come home and find me there asking questions."

"What do we do?"

She leaned forward and wrapped her arm around my shoulder, "Anything we can do to protect Cathy. Over my dead body will Lucas ever hurt her again."

I wanted to be comforted in that, but the idea of my mom dying was more like an omen than a phrase.

*

As I alternated between a grilled cheese and finishing my case notes, I couldn't help but notice how Macy kept looking up at me. She was squinting her eyes and then staring at her hand. Her eyes kept widening, and she was gaping like a fish.

"Okay, I give up. What the heck are you doing?" I asked, laying down my folders and raising my eyebrows at her.

Macy laughed, "I'm sorry. I know you're trying to work."

"Yes, I have a ton of notes to finish. And you staring at your hands like you're stoned isn't helping. Are you stoned?"

"No!"

"Then what?"

She leaned forward, a giddy grin on her face, "The auras are getting stronger. When I started seeing them last year, they were barely halos around people's heads, and I could see pastel colors only. Now all around the color is solid. I can see you Terry, the color of your soul."

"Really? Mac, that's amazing. Have you told Mom?"

She shook her head, "Not yet. I was waiting for it to get stronger. I keep trying to see if I can see my own."

"Can you?"

"No! And I want to. I have a theory. The color of your aura can tell a lot about your personality. What if I could help people find the love of their life based on them? That's kind of foolproof?!"

"But how will you figure out which ones are compatible?"

She waved her hand at me, "In time, sister dear. But just think what that means for you!"

"What does that mean for me?"

"You could be my first match! You could be my first success story, and I could do a toast at your wedding about how I put you two together and found romance for you."

"I haven't even met anyone yet, and you are already talking about a wedding? Who says that I want to date right now?"

Macy rolled her eyes, "Who doesn't want to fall in love? I think you are holding back because you are terrified of what happened to Mom and Dad. But if I helped you pick that person then it would basically be a sure thing."

I leaned forward a little, "I am not holding back. I have a lot going on right now. Patients rely on me. I have more important things to worry about right now than romance."

She sighed and sat back in her chair, defeated.

"But, how about this. When I am ready to find out who my aura is seeking out, I will let you know first. I will let you set me up. You are allowed to speak at my hypothetical wedding."

Macy grinned, "Deal! That gives me time to do some research."

I laughed but had a nagging feeling in my chest as I went back to my files. Was I holding back? I knew that the Gina situation was life and death, but on some level, I knew there was always going to be a case that was like this.

My job was always going to pair me up with relationships that dominated my life so that I could save them. But what about my personal life? Was I allowing myself to be paired up?

If Macy found my perfect color compliment, would I be willing to let go enough to give myself a chance to find happiness? Would I even be given a chance?

Chapter Four

Claire
June 2015

I can't stop staring at my IV. I felt like if I stared at my punctured arm long enough, I would suddenly learn how I got to the hospital.

I was not wearing my jeans and button up anymore. At some point, someone got me into a hospital gown instead. It was too big and kept falling off of my shoulder. My wrist was bandaged, and my fingers were numb and painful.

I moved gingerly, and the throb informed me that my wrist was more than sprained. I tried to stand to find my mom, but my head started swimming, and I had to grasp the bed rails. As my feet hung over the edge, I thought back to the crash and the breath that I had felt.

Despite myself, I leaned over the hospital bed to see if those black smudges somehow made their way to wherever I was. The tile is shiny and reflects the fluorescent lights back into my eyes.

I closed my eyes, feeling the asphalt under my hands and seeing Terry crumpled up in my lap. Had we gotten in an ambulance? When had they separated us? Did my mom follow in another ambulance?

The sound of the door opening forced my eyelids apart, and I saw Macy at the front of the bed. She was trembling, and her face was a shade of purple that I have never seen on skin before.

"Macy…." My voice caught in my throat as she gently climbed into bed with me.

I wrapped my arms around her and let myself accept the moment before thinking past it. I wanted to hold her and not think about why we were crying. It was too much, to think about why she was the only one here with me.

"Did they tell you anything?" she asked quietly.

"I don't think so. I don't even remember being checked in. I remember... Being there and waking up here."

"You were hysterical. The nurse had to sedate you to put the IV in."

I shivered, uncomfortable with them touching me after I was unconscious.

"Did they tell you anything?"

She shook her head lightly, "Not much. I haven't seen anyone else. I am not 18, they called Dad, and he is on his way."

I took a shaky breath, something about Dad trying to sign paperwork for Mom made my stomach hurt. I couldn't even remember the last time they talked face to face, let alone discussed insurance. A small knock on the door followed a nurse popping her head in.

"The police need to ask you a few questions. Are you up for that?"

I assented, holding Macy closer so that they wouldn't try to send her away. Two male police officers came in and went through some easy questions like my name and where we had dinner earlier that night.

"Now, do you remember anything strange about the drive home?" I covered my eyes, trying to focus.

"No, we had just come from dinner. My sister Terry won an award this week for her work as a social worker, and we were celebrating. I loaned Macy my car so that she could go to a football game with a friend."

Macy let out a sniffle as I talked about her asking to use my car. If I had been driving her as I wanted, then both of us would have been safe.

"We were singing along to the radio and stopped at a red light. There were no other cars at the intersection except for a truck stopped on our left-hand side."

I opened my eyes, realizing something.

"But he was stopped at a green light.... We were at the stop light, and he had the go-ahead. He could have gone ahead of us. But he waited for our light to turn green then rammed into us. He ran us off the road. He hit us from the left-hand side, where Terry was sitting. He hit us."

"Did your sister notice him waiting?"

I shook my head, "No, she was looking at me through the rearview mirror. I was upset about something at dinner, and she was trying to cheer me up. I only noticed him because I thought I saw the truck at dinner earlier, it was a rundown truck. I remember thinking how strange it was to see a truck that beat up in the parking lot with so many beautiful cars surrounding it. Then seeing it again on the road hours later."

As the police left, Macy pulled back from me to talk.

"You think someone did it on purpose?"

"There's no other way to explain it. He waited for a least a minute, waiting for our light to be green and for us to drive into the intersection. Then he gunned it. The squeal of the tires scared Terry, she jumped and tried to speed up to get us out of the way."

I laid back on the bed.

Terry was the most caring person in the entire world. She wanted to fix everyone's problems even if it meant suffering herself. Who could have hated her enough to try to kill us?

Terry

One Month Before
May 2015

"I think you need more than just a couch and a coffee table that you made by duct taping pizza boxes together," I told CJ, stepping closer to the display to open the drawers of an entertainment center at Target.

"The pizzable is not the most amazing thing you have ever seen?" he asked, raising his eyebrows at me.

"You have to quit calling it a pizzable. If you name it, then you will not be able to let go when I finally get it into a dumpster."

"Answer the question, Terry!"

I sighed, smiling, "Yes, CJ. Your pizza table was very creative. But you are an adult. An adult that can afford furniture. It's time to start living in the present."

He grimaced but grabbed the furniture catalog off of the display. My phone buzzed in my pocket. It was a number I didn't recognize.

"Hello?"

"Hi, is this Terry Shaw? I'm calling on behalf of Gina Carlton."

I was listed as her emergency contact. She was in the hospital yet again. I drove to the emergency room in a daze, barely seeing the road in front of me. As I found Gina's room, I had to fight back nausea as I worried about what kind of shape, she would be in.

A nurse was still attaching the IV to her arm with a thin strip of tape. Both of her eyes were swollen, and she had a nasty gash on her collarbone that looked like it was going to need stitches. From the appearance of her shoulder wrapped in an Ace bandage, he had broken yet another one of her bones.

"Shoulder or collarbone?" I asked softly, sitting on the edge of her bed.

Her eyes were dulled from pain pills, but she finally found my face.

"Shoulder blade. He cracked my shoulder blade and broke two of my ribs."

"Gina, when did you go back? You were doing so well."

She looked down, crying softly.

"My garbage disposal broke, and the sink kept filling up with this disgusting water. I couldn't call my brother. He used to co-own the house with me, but we had a falling out over Lucas more than a year ago. So, I called Lucas and asked if he could fix it while I was at work. He did. He came in, he left, and he brought me some beautiful flowers. They had a card asking me to dinner that night."

I held her hand as she looked up, she was begging me to understand.

"He hasn't done that for so long. Since before things changed between us. I started to see a piece of who he used to be. We went to dinner, and it was incredible. He barely kissed me goodbye that night. So, I asked him to dinner the next night, at home. I wanted to cook for him. While he was over, he asked me about our wedding plans. I told him I wasn't sure it was the right time to talk about our future and he just…. snapped."

My stomach clenched, knowing what came next.

"I ran to the bathroom, trying to grab the phone on the way. He smacked it out of my hand. I made it to the bathroom. He ripped the shower curtain off the hooks and used it to choke me. At one point… It was covering my face… I couldn't breathe," Gina started to shake, her words seeming to jerk out of her chest as she spoke.

I leaned forward, gently putting my hand over hers. I wanted to hold her but was afraid of hurting her even more.

"Are you going to go back?" I whispered.

She shook her head furiously, wincing as she jostled her arm. "I used to think he needed me. His parents had him when they were older and passed away right after he graduated from high school. He would always tell me I was his family and I liked being needed. But… I can't be his everything. I don't want to be that for him anymore. No. I need to stay at the shelter. Maybe even a different one that he doesn't know about it. It was different this time."

"How? Were you afraid for your life? We've been there before."

"Not only my life," Gina whispered.

My skin broke out in chills, my stomach dropping. I had this strange sense of déjà vu that had never happened before. I saw the past but never was part of those visions. Everything had already happened, and I was just there to help pick up the pieces.

I had always been part of the past and had yet to piece together what my role was in the future.

"Have I ever told you about my mom?" Gina said, looking up at me strangely.

"No," I said, feeling like I was somehow giving something away.

Maybe she recognized my mom from the photos in my office. Maybe she was trying to reach out in a way she was unable to do when my mom came to talk to her.

"My mom had a... Accident a few years ago. She had dementia and started to deteriorate quickly. She needed to go to a nursing home. It's expensive... But she's my mom. I want to do everything possible to make her life better. I can't take care of her 24/7 and still take care of the house she left me. But I can work my ass off to pay for the best help possible. I can get a better job if Lucas is out of the picture. I can do it all on my own."

When she talked about Cathy, her voice took on a ferocity that I had never heard before.

"Does Lucas agree with the... arrangement? I guess that your mom wasn't a fan of him when you all lived together."

Gina began jabbering, "You're right. The abuse started when my mom, Cathy, started getting worse. She took up a lot of my time and Lucas was jealous. Now, he is resentful of the money that I spend on her care. He pays for most of it, and that's another reason why I was always terrified of cutting him out completely."

"What would he rather you do?" I asked, feeling the words come out of my mouth like they had shape.

If this was a court TV show the defense side would be yelling, "Leading!"

Gina locked eyes with me, "He wants my mom to either go to a state home or for my brother to take care of her. He thinks that the wedding planning is taking longer because I am being held back by her condition. He is ready to start a life without her in it."

"And what do you think?"

"It's time for me to start my life without Lucas."

I let out a deep breath, relieved. As much as I wanted to think that we were somehow able to warn Gina of the future soon enough to help change it, a deep sadness came over me that I couldn't shake.

*

I was shuffling the files I need to take home and organize when I walked into Olive Grove. I needed to talk to my mom, to tell her about Gina's injuries and try to figure out our next step.

As I round the hallway to where my mom's nursing station is, I see her standing next to a cart outside of a room. She briefly catches my eye, and suddenly I feel a force coming from her, warning me not to interrupt her.

My eyes fell to the man in front of her, who was gesturing angrily. I realized it was Lucas and slipped into an empty room so that I could keep an eye on her without him seeing me.

"I know it was you that came to the house. I found your card hidden next to the crockpot. What did you want? Even more money?"

I was surprised that Gina had kept my mom's card. She doesn't have them printed for her nursing job but rather to hand out to people that might require her less than traditional services.

"No, our center has all the money it needs to provide Cathy's care. Why would you think that I was somehow trying to extort from her?"

"Because she hid it. The only thing we fight about is money. It couldn't be about anything else."

My mom's eyes shone like steel, "That's the only thing you fight about?"

My stomach flip-flopped. I knew what he had done to Gina. I was pretty sure that Lucas wouldn't try anything in the middle of a busy

42

nursing home but still wanted to snatch my mom away. Lucas shuffled, looking down for a moment before puffing himself up again.

"Yes, that's the only thing. I love Gina. What I don't love is how you nosy bitches here are taking advantage of her and her family. You charge an arm and a leg for sponge baths so that you can rifle through people's wallets while they sleep."

"Not only is that ridiculous, but centers like this are necessary for families that can't take care of their parents or want better for them. Gina cares about her mother and Olive Grove is the best aging and long-term care housing in town."

"I'm sure."

My mom stepped up to him, pulling herself up to her whole height of 5'2. It would have been funny if it wasn't so terrifying.

"What would your alternative be? Take her home? Spend your days and nights making sure she gets the best care possible?"

Lucas shook his head shortly, "No. And I don't think I am going to have to worry about this place for much longer either. I believe that nature will take its course sooner than later."

"Is that a threat?"

Lucas shrugged, "Old people die all the time. It's a pity that it usually happens while they are alone."

My mom's mouth thinned to a white line; she looked ready to sock him. Before she could say another word, he turned and strode down the hallway.

I took a deep breath and joined my mom, dropping my bag to pull her into a hug. She was trembling, but I knew that it was from anger and not fear.

"I have never touched such an evil person before. It radiated off of him. I was coming to give patients their afternoon medicine and caught him trying to get into Cathy's room. It was empty, thank God, she is getting physical therapy right now."

"Well, that's a blessing. What did he think he was going to achieve here in the middle of the day? He came from beating Gina almost to death to finish the job on her mom?"

My mom's eyes widened, "Gina? Is she okay?"

43

I shrugged, "She will be in the hospital for a few days at the very least. She likes to check herself out against medical advice. Afterward, she is staying at a private shelter. I think this was the final straw. She broke emotionally. She told me that they were fighting over Cathy's care. She said that he was ready to cut ties and finally start their own life."

"By one force of nature or another?"

"Does this count as a threat? Are we able to call the police now? We can't let him sneak back in and hurt her. Once he is finished with Cathy, he is going to find a way to get rid of Gina. He won't stop until all the money and power are his alone."

"No police yet."

"Why not?"

"I have no witnesses to his statements; he didn't see Cathy. All we can do now is hope Gina presses charges against him and puts him in jail for as long as possible. We need some time to make a plan."

I picked my bag back up, thinking of Gina's file inside. She had never pressed charges before. She had seemed so sure of her Lucas free future, but would that resolve fade along with her injuries?

Would she finally seek a restraining order? Especially now that she feared for more than just herself, knowing that her mom's life was hanging in the balance as well. Abuse was such a confusing cat and mouse game for the victims.

It broke my heart that there was so much collateral damage and that Gina would have a hand in her mom's death if she couldn't stand firm.

*

Macy had recently told me that she didn't know how we did it, exposing ourselves to people's pain every single day. When I think about it, I never had a choice.

Growing up, I began to notice a pattern to my visions. I rarely saw the good things from a person's past. For the most part, it was the days of their life that they wanted to keep hidden from

44

everyone. I finally understood that trauma is usually repeated and that leaves a residual hue to people's spirits.

Something about my gift made that kind of pain the easiest for me to see. If I could see pain so clearly, shouldn't my lifelong goal be to bring balance to that pain? If I had only been able to see the happiness of a person's life, how could I add to that in a way that would make the world a better place?

The only way for me to make my corner of the world brighter is to weed through the darkest parts. If I am supposed to be bringing balance to my life, does that mean I have to do something good with a curse?

If this was truly a "gift," would I even be able to see this darkness?

Chapter Five

Claire
June 2015

"Terry is finally out of surgery," Macy said, coming back into my room after talking to the doctor out in the hall.

I sat forward, voracious for information. Since I was still a patient, everyone was trying to treat me like I was made of papier-mache. They were afraid that if they kept me updated that I would go into shock and need to stay there longer.

But waiting and feeling out of the loop was even worse than not being able to go home.

"How does she seem?" I asked.

"I haven't seen her yet. They have her in recovery. But there's something more," she cried quietly as she sat on the edge of my bed.

"What? The surgery went badly?"

She shook her head, "I heard them talking to Dad. The surgery went well, but Terry hasn't woken up yet. The anesthesia wore off; she should be awake by now. Her body is healing, but her mind doesn't seem to be coming along as quickly."

"What does that mean?"

"It means that they aren't sure she is going to wake up."

I looked at my blanket, bunched between my scratched fingers and knuckles.

"What if she doesn't?"

Macy launched herself into my arms.

"The doctor said, full disclosure like he was some cheesy journalist. He told Dad that Terry had specified in her insurance that she didn't want to be on life support or a similar state for more than 90 days. That if she were in that condition, she wanted no life-saving precautions."

"What?!"

Anger surged through my body. I vaguely remembered a conversation from high school when we were talking about physician-assisted suicide.

Terry had said that she didn't believe our gifts would be quieted even if her body was too weak to respond. She was hated the idea of her gift wrestling with her consciousness and her body living in a state of scared exhaustion.

I remembered, but I didn't want to. Macy's tears soaked the front of my shirt.

"What about Mom?"

Terry

May 2015

"Lucy, if Gina calls back could you please have her call my cell phone directly?" I said, picking my purse off of my desk and heading out of the office with Macy.

"A problem with a patient?" Macy asked, shoving her phone into the pocket of her overly tight jeans.

I sighed, wanting to tell her about the situation more than anything. Lucas' behavior creeped me out, but mom didn't want to worry her if it came to nothing. Today was a rare afternoon off for me, and we were using to buy a graduation present for Claire.

"There's always a problem. Otherwise, they wouldn't need my help to begin with," I said, taking a deep breath.

"I just don't get it. I feel like I would have the hardest time not telling patients off. Some people are hell-bent on driving themselves into the ground."

"That's a little harsh, Mac. Needing that kind of relationship from someone usually stems from an awful home life growing up. It's hard to get out of."

She nodded distractedly, flipping through CDs angrily.

"Is this about my job? Or are you not in the mood to shop for Claire right now?" I asked, turning to face her.

"It might be a little bit about Claire."

I sighed, thinking about her rant. "

Hell-bent on driving herself into the ground. She seems to be doing okay."

"That's not the point! It's that she is doing it without us! Mom is so excited to see her graduate, and I feel like Claire doesn't give a crap. She wants to do everything on her own, and our lives are completely separate."

I didn't want to agree with her, but it was too close to home to dismiss entirely.

"I have a hard time understanding her, too."

Macy raised her eyebrow at me, "Do you remember how close we all were? Why does she get to be more upset about the divorce than us?"

I did remember. Barbie marathons and watching movies until 2 am. Her reading her current book to us and having us make predictions about where the plot would lead. Giving each other ridiculous makeovers and dancing in front of the mirror.

A million memories that felt like they happened to another group of sisters altogether.

"I think it's more than that. It's the gifts. We have them, and it helps us understand Mom more. She doesn't have one, so it's easier to pretend like we are nuts and she is the special one."

Mac snorted, looking upset. I stepped forward and kissed her on the forehead.

"We are sisters, Mac. We love each other with all of the good and the bad. Life stages come in waves, and you sometimes have to wade out really far to figure out who you are. But sooner than later, you always end up back on the beach. We will always find each other in life. I promise."

*

"Terry, someone's here to see you," Lucy said, her voice stilted over the phone.

"A patient?"

"I don't think so."

With my heart quickening, I went out into the lobby, where a tall man with light hair was standing next to Lucy's desk. Her tight smile revealed that even she was affected by his overwhelming presence.

"Hi, can I help you?" I asked, trying to mask my emotions.

"Yes, my name is Lucas. I am Gina's fiancé, and she told me that you are her counselor. I would like to speak to you."

I took him in, attempting to control my emotions as I put a face to the name I had heard too often from Gina. I jerked my head forward and spread my hands in a go-ahead gesture.

49

"In private."

I gave Lucy a look but allowed Lucas to follow me back to my office. When he sat in the chair across from my desk, I made a point of leaving the door open.

"Does this seem private?" Lucas asked, smirking at me.

"Let me make myself clear. As Gina's counselor, I have been made aware of the kind of person you are. The door stays open, or you can see yourself out."

He glared at me, "Fine. But I think it's crap that I am being painted as this awful person."

"What did you need to talk to me about," I asked, ignoring his pity party.

He leaned forward, attempting to look grave and calm.

"I am worried about Gina."

I snorted, "Me too. Someone beat her up, and now she is in the hospital."

Lucas' eyes flashed, but he pushed ahead.

"I think the real issue is her situation with her mom. It's very complicated. Her brother has been coming around more and trying to get involved, but it's clear he has other motives."

"Like what?"

"Well, two years ago he was taken out of their moms will because he is a drunk and hit Cathy."

My hands were clammy as I laid them on my lap, "He hit their mom? Is that why she is in a nursing home?"

"No, she has dementia. But the stress of the situation was a contributing factor. Tom is money hungry and doesn't care who gets in the way. I am worried that he is going to come after Gina and force her to add him to the will so he can support his addiction."

"I am under the impression that their mother isn't deceased. Why would he come after her now?"

Lucas sat back in his chair, his dominance trying to creep its way over to my side of the room.

"Their mother is elderly and sick. It's only a matter of time."

50

His words made me sick as did his nonchalance. I wanted him gone.

"You know, I find this cycle just fascinating. Gina had a brother who was abusive, maybe a father. It's strange that women who know better usually decide to spend their lives with the wrong people, especially in romantic relationships."

"You mean me? Am I wrong for Gina? I am the best thing that has ever happened to that girl."

I stood and extended my hand, eager to read him and never see him again. Lucas stared me down before standing and taking my hand. I steeled myself as a compelling vision shook me.

But instead of a man holding a pillow over Cathy's face, she was younger. I saw her bleeding from the mouth and a young man standing over her. A man that was not Lucas.

"You might have been the best thing about her past. But her future is going to be a lot better."

Lucas snatched his hand back, and it was clear that he wanted to push me away or even slap me. Instead, he spat on my black flats and strode out of the office.

"Do you want me to call the police?" Lucy asked, looking frightened.

"Yes, but don't let yourself get upset. I can handle him. He's a coward. They all are Lucy. Remember that. Nothing is more cowardly than hitting someone that loves you. Those men all end up self-destructing."

I squeezed her shoulder and returned to my office. I sat, shaking a little before I had to get up and pretend to need the restroom so that I could wash my hands. I wanted none of Lucas on my skin.

I wanted to shed the situation like bubbles down the drain.

*

"You called the police?" my mom's voice tightened even over the phone.

"Yes, Mom. Not the emergency line. The one to ask questions. I told them the situation, and they filed a report."

51

"How much did you tell them?"

"The whole thing. The visions. His creepy behavior. My fear for Gina and Cathy."

"What did they say?"

"Of course, they thought I was nuts. But at least it's on file somewhere just in case."

"Just in case?!"

"Yes, Mom. Just in case. He is the one who is nuts. I am trying to hold it together, but he scares the crap out of me."

"I don't want rumors to start about you and your credibility to be shot if you ever need to make a report on behalf of our patients."

My stomach bottomed out as I accepted how true her words were.

Would I ever be taken seriously again? Would I become known as some kind of dial a psychic whose hobby was counseling abuse victims? Would people assume I was a crackpot who preyed on vulnerable populations to take advantage of them?

"Mom, he came here and was very threatening. Even Lucy was afraid. She witnessed him spitting on me. That alone counts as harassment. If I can't help Gina press charges at least the police are aware that he has tried intimidating us."

She finally agreed with me but filing a report made this more concrete than either of us wanted it to be. I wondered how many more reports would have to be filed. I wondered if it would help at all.

*

"What's the plan?" I asked my mom.

"I need forms for Cathy's insurance signed, and Gina is still in the hospital. Tom is listed as the secondary emergency contact, so I need his help. You are Gina's friend, and we are trying to get some information."

I rubbed my hands together nervously as we headed up the stairs of a dilapidated apartment building to unit 23. I knocked on the door and heard rustling. As the door opened, I was stunned by how much Tom looked like Gina.

The shape of their eyes, the color of their hair, even the tilt of their lips that hinted at a shy grin.

"Hi, I hope I have the right apartment. Are you Tom Carlton?"

He frowned, standing up straighter with an anxious expression.

"Well, my name is Marlo, and this is Terry. I am from Olive Grove Retirement, where your mom is being taken care of. I have some insurance forms I need to go over with you."

Tom shuffled his feet, "I think that my sister is the emergency contact for my mom."

My mom smiled softly, "Yes. But the situation is a little bit complicated. May we come in to discuss this privately?"

He hesitated before swinging the door open and leading us to a small living room. The room was decorated sparsely with an old couch and top of the line TV on a garage sale entertainment shelf.

"Complicated? Are they okay?" Tom asked.

My mom sat on the couch, and I joined her. Tom grabbed a fold out chair from the kitchen and sat across from us.

"Your mother's dementia is worsening, and the insurance forms need to be updated to keep her care continuous. Gina usually handles these issues but is currently in the hospital."

His eyes narrowed, "In the hospital? What did he do?"

I gave my mom a look, unsure how much to reveal.

"She was beaten if you are implying that," I said quietly.

Tom ran his fingers through his hair angrily, "Yes. I know all about that."

He stood, beginning to pace.

"You know about Lucas?"

"Oh yeah. I know about that dickhead. It's his fault that I am unable to help. I was kicked out the house once they started dating. Lucas wants the whole estate for himself and wants Mom and me out of the way. He has been hitting Gina for years, but she refuses to press charges. The last time I called the police, they didn't believe me. Lucas can be so freaking charming."

"The whole estate?" my mom asked.

Tom looked at his feet, sitting back down.

"I used to have a drinking problem. Actually, I still do. I go to meetings, but the guilt makes it hard to shake. I stole money from her. My mom. And when she confronted me, I pushed her. I was coming off a bender and hysterical. She hit her mouth on the counter, and her tooth went through. She had to get stitches. It was right before her diagnosis. Lucas convinced her that I was dangerous and that I would murder her to steal her money. My mom was losing her grip on reality quickly and disinherited me."

My stomach dropped. At the same time, alcoholism is unpredictable. Addicts could be very charming to get what they wanted.

Could we trust him? Lucas could have used that weakness to remove him from the situation. He had admitted he was still drinking.

"I am going to be honest. Lucas told me that he is claiming that he is now worried for Gina's life," I said, trying to feel out the truth.

Tom's eyes bulged, either in anger or fear that we knew the truth.

"That's insane. After hitting my mom, I considered that my rock bottom. The next day I checked myself into rehab. Lucas hand-delivered the new will to me and told me never to contact them again. I have kept to their wishes except to send them cards on their birthday."

My mom gave him a sympathetic pat and laid a hand over his. After getting Tom to update the paperwork, we said goodbye. All of my snapshots from him were blurry; I assumed it was from the alcohol he was still trying to shake. He was a mess.

"What do you think?" my mom asked as she buckled in beside me.

"I want to believe him. I feel like if Gina were afraid of him, it would have come up our sessions."

"I received pure anger when I touched him. But I didn't see anything with him and Cathy in the same room."

"He could still be the person who caused her stroke, but he might not be the person who plans to hurt her in the future."

"Well, the future is flexible."

"So, it could be good. Or it could mean that he just hasn't decided to hurt her yet."

My mom shrugged, looking defeated.

How do you investigate a murder that hasn't happened yet?

Chapter Six

Claire
June 2015

Ripping my IV out should have sent searing pain through my arm, but any pain I felt was now was secondary to my heart. As my dad kept talking it seemed like he was unaware of the fact that I was escaping from my bed.

"She didn't make it. There was nothing they could do; I was told over and over that it was upon impact and that she felt no pain. The ambulance could have been parked right next to you guys, and it wouldn't have been soon enough."

"No, that's not possible. Because I was there. I held her in my arms... I am sure I felt her breathing..."

Macy shook her head, wrapping herself up in her arms and rocking in the bed.

My dad stared at us both helplessly, so lost in how to help us. I wondered if he was smothered with the realization that he was our only parent now. That he alone was responsible for our well-being.

"No, Claire. She died immediately. You should take comfort in that."

I pushed him in anger, "Take comfort? How dare you."

As I forced myself out of the room, I thought back to the accident. I thought back to dragging myself out of the twisted metal and pulling her out of her seat. I squeezed my eyes shut, trying to focus despite my hammering heart.

She was breathing! I could have sworn she was breathing.

My stomach dropped as I remembered that I had felt the breath, but it wasn't coming from my mother's mouth or nose. It was on the back of my neck. I tried to make sense of it, but the breath had most definitely been coming from behind me.

Suddenly terrified of the dark behind my eyelids, I forced my eyes open. The previously sparse hallway was suddenly crowded.

Black spots swam in my vision. The air around me looked like it was made of wax paper. So many people, wearing hospital gowns of all colors and styles. Searching. Moaning and holding their various injuries as they stumbled about.

"Claire?" Macy poked her head out of the door and locked eyes with me.

How quickly her eyes found me convinced me of what I already had suspected. She couldn't see anyone else in the hall. We were the only ones here. My veil was dissolving with every beat of my heart.

I screamed as I fell into the darkness of my eyelids once more, afraid of what laid in the pitch black now that it was torn open.

Terry

June 2015

For as long as I can remember, my mom stressed how important it was to keep our gift close to our heart. We couldn't share it with too many people because it was unusual and sometimes hard to understand. Only people that loved us would be able to accept it and be part of our life and our journey.

But sometimes circumstance forced out our secret so that we could help people. So that we could warn them.

I had reached that point with Gina. She was living out of the hospital, and I was so scared for her. I was so worried that she would cave in once more and let Lucas back into her life. That he would finally kill her.

As she sat across from me, I tried to put what I wanted to say into simple words.

"Part of my job is being perceptive to people and their lives. I need to know things about them so that I can help them in the best way possible" I started, awkwardly crossing my legs.

It had been a long time since I had been in the situation where someone could choose to think I was a crazy psychic. It was daunting.

"Okay. Like asking me questions I might not want to answer?" Gina said, picking up on my strange mood.

"Yes. Kind of like that. But sometimes it goes much deeper for me. When I... touch someone, I can receive something that they didn't tell me. And that helps me help them."

My palms sweated as Gina stared at me.

"Receive something? What? Like a vibe?"

I sighed, knowing I had to give her the full story.

"A couple of months ago I had a vision. I saw a senior woman being hurt by someone. I think he was trying to kill her. And I also believe that woman is your mother."

Gina's mouth dropped open, and her cheeks grew red.

"Are you kidding me?"

"No, I am trying to warn you. I have been trying to help you. Lucas even came here, trying to get me to leave you alone. I have this awful feeling that he is going to hurt you and your mom."

I leaned forward, attempting to squeeze her hand.

"Don't touch me!" she said, snatching her hand away and standing.

"Gina, please don't freak out. This is okay. We can work together."

"No, no we can't. You are crazy; you know that right?! What do you want? Money for you to 'save' my family. No thanks. Leave me alone."

My vision swam, and tears choked my throat.

"Of course not. I don't want anything. I just want to help. I can't stand by and watch you be hurt."

Gina grabbed her purse and glared at me, "I am not going to get hurt. Honestly, stay away from me. I don't need this. I don't need your help or your psychic visions. I don't need anyone to save me. You're nuts, and you're not going to manipulate me."

I followed her as far as the lobby before she threatened to call the police for a restraining order. Lucy's mouth hung open as I walked back to my office and shut the door.

Hiding my head in my arms, I let myself cry before calling my mom.

*

"Okay, call me when you are ready for a ride home tomorrow morning."

I could hear Macy sigh from over the phone. Mom was out tonight with her best friend Missy, and it looked like Macy was spending the night with a friend to cram for the last tests of the year.

"I'm serious, Mac. Study. You only have a couple of weeks left of school."

After saying goodbye, I hung up my cell phone and looked up at the dark house waiting for me. Taking a deep breath, I opened the car door and walked to our gate.

A soft mewling echoed through the empty yard, giving me chills. I looked around, the shadows already long and dark.

"Hello?" I called out, not wanting to draw any attention to myself.

There was no response, so I quietly opened the gate and started up the path. The mewling echoed again, coming from the backyard.

I remembered Macy finding a kitten caught in a rainstorm last summer and us having to bring it to the pound. She would die if there were another half starving litter under the porch. I slipped my phone into my pocket and made my way to the backyard.

It was almost too hard to see, and I contemplated going inside for a flashlight, but the mewling was getting louder. My foot bumped into something soft, and I carefully bent down to examine it.

A calico cat, torn open, laid on the grass. My mouth filled with bile as I saw the intestines pulled from the open belly, and the cat's eyes rolled up at me.

It tried to writhe closer to me, and I recoiled.

It was wearing a collar, how had it gotten here? What the hell happened to it? I shrugged off my sweater and carefully tried covering the mutilated animal.

The gate closed with a clang. Fear saturated my body as I took in the situation.

I had come into the dark backyard willingly. This cat was a message.

I took a deep shuddering breath before bolting to the back porch. Someone slipped on the wet grass and cursed angrily. My mom usually left the back door open. I flew through it, locking it behind me.

Footsteps thundered onto the porch, and the doorknob wiggled. I covered my mouth with my hand, frozen. Three loud thumps rattled the door and then it was quiet.

I realized that my purse was still on the front porch. I had files in my bag, Gina's records with her last safe house address. As I walked through the living room, my arms began shaking.

Somehow, I had grabbed the cat when I stood to run, and it was struggling in my hands. It bit at me, and a strand of intestine fell through my sweater and left a glistening line on my forearm.

I screamed, dropping it. My purse still sat on the porch hidden in the shadows. I could easily open the door to grab it but couldn't force myself to move.

The mangled cat crawled around behind me, its pained call making me want to vomit. The blood trailing across the floor looked ludicrous on my mom's clean carpet. This didn't match my life.

But my life would never be the same again; someone had been watching me. Someone was still watching me. I would never be alone again.

*

"CJ, please. I am not ready to talk about Gina again," I said.

I pulled my slippers over my feet and settled onto the couch for a Disney movie marathon. Over the last two days, I couldn't stop showering. In between bathing sessions, I binged Disney to disassociate.

CJ had buried the cat, but I still felt its open body against my chest. I didn't even ask where my sweater was now. CJ had agreed to stay with us until all of this was settled.

"This is only half about Gina," CJ said, sitting next to me and unfolding a newspaper.

"She doesn't want my help. What am I supposed to do?"

"Just read it," he laid the newspaper on my lap.

Rolling my eyes, I lifted it and was surprised to see that it was the obituary pages.

Tom Carlton passed away on Thursday. He is survived by his mother, Cathy and sister Gina. The service is to be held on Saturday at the One Heart Baptist Church at 1 pm.

"CJ, what does this mean? Did Lucas kill him?! I didn't see any of this?!"

He shrugged, "What if this is over? What if he is the one who was going to try to smother Cathy and the guilt of almost killing her put him over the edge? It could have been Tom this whole time. Maybe you weren't supposed to prevent anything. Have you ever wondered if you are meant to help them put the pieces back together?"

My job was helping people after the trauma happened, it was never to prevent it from happening. Maybe I was meant to find Gina, to help her reinvent herself and move on.

As shocked as I was, I wanted that to be true. I let myself fall apart from relief, collapsing into CJ's arms.

*

"Congratulations again," Macy told me, hugging me tightly then going to Claire to beg to use her car one last time.

We had finished the party celebrating my award and frankly, I was exhausted. The actual event was boring. Afterward, we had dinner with my mom and sisters, one of which was super quiet and grouchy all evening.

Claire seemed to have news of her own that she didn't want to share. I was emotionally and physically drained, I just wanted to get home and take a bath.

"Are you sure you don't want to go out?" CJ asked, helping me carry my gifts to my car.

"No, I am tuckered out. Did you see them in there?" I asked.

CJ glanced over to my family, where Macy was begging Claire, and my mom was trying to smile at them encouragingly.

"Yeah. It was tense. Which is why I want to take you out for a real celebration."

I sighed and looked out to the street. At the stop light, I saw a truck that I made me stop short.

I immediately recognized it as Lucas's and was filled with a dull anger. I was angry with everything this award meant, what had to happen to these women for them to seek help from my center.

I did deserve to celebrate. Because Lucas was alone in that truck, seething as he locked eyes with me. Cathy was safe; Gina was safe. Because of me.

Why shouldn't I celebrate that?

"Hey, Macy's going to use my car to go out with Britney. Do you mind dropping me off at Dads?" Claire asked.

"Yeah, that's fine," I said absently.

"So?" CJ said.

"Let me drop them off, and I will meet you at Tilly's. We will go dancing and get some drinks. I have earned it."

He gave me a squeeze, "Yes, you have. See you in an hour."

Isn't strange that even as a psychic, I had no idea this would be the last night I spent with them? No one has any idea when they are going to be confronted with death.

Chapter Seven

Claire
June 2015

"Is it all done?" Macy asked quietly as I finished my call with Lawson and Sons funeral home.

"The service is set for Tuesday at one."

Macy bit her lip, "So it's finished."

I cradled my broken wrist awkwardly, wishing I knew how to comfort her. I was numb and out of touch. I thought back to holding her in the hospital and wondered why I wasn't able to do it now.

This was my fault, this accident, this distance. I wished I could trade places with Terry, I deserved to be broken. She would know how to make everyone feel better in this impossible situation.

"It's not all finished... I got a call from Mom's lawyer yesterday. He wanted to know if we were using her house. I wasn't sure how long we would need to get you moved out."

Macy's eyes widened and overflowed, "I am not going anywhere. That is my home. The home I had with Mom."

"Mac, I get that. But you can't live alone. And we can't ask Dad to move back in."

"No, but I can ask you."

"What? Me? You want me to be your guardian? How is that going to seem to Dad? The only thing that makes sense is for you to be here."

"You can't wait to run away again! When are you planning on leaving? Will you even wait until after the funeral?"

My face burned, "This isn't about me. This is about you being a spoiled brat."

"Screw you. I'm going home."

"Is it Dad?" I asked, confused and angry.

"You know what, yeah. It is. I don't want to live here. I want to be in my house. Where I grew up with the only family that cared

64

about me. I will stay there until Terry is okay again. She will take care of me. It's clear you have no interest in helping me out."

"That's bullshit. You are 17. You need to be with a parent."

"That's right. I am 17. It's only a year. I don't need you or him."

"Do you really hate him that much? He is all we have left. You are not an adult. This is not a decision for you to make!" I yelled, pushing Macy back onto the couch.

"You really don't get it, Claire. I love Dad, it's him that doesn't love me!"

I stepped back, feeling like I was physically slapped.

"What are you talking about? Of course, he loves you. He is our dad."

"No, he's your dad. He never accepted me. I can't live there Claire; it will kill me. I can't be someone I am not for a year. I will slowly die; I swear to God."

"Macy, you are ridiculous. He accepts you. He loves you. He already knows about your gift. He doesn't hate you for it, it just scares him."

"That's not the part of me I am talking about!" Macy screamed, forcing me to take another step back.

Seeing the tears well in her eyes, I remembered every afternoon we spent playing Barbie's. The time she skinned her knee riding my brand-new bike that was too big for her and how I began to cry like I could feel it myself.

I wrapped my arms around her. She tried to struggle and then went limp in my arms as she started to sob.

"Just tell me," I asked.

She shook her head frantically. I thought back to her pleads, saying that she would die living with my dad. What could be so bad?

"Macy, please. I love you just as you are. Tell me how to help."

She looked up at me, her eyes huge.

"Come live with me. Let me finish my senior year in my high school, don't make me leave my home."

My eyebrows furrowed, "It's not a school that is making you this upset."

Macy looked down again, guarded. I held her at arm's length, so she had to make eye contact.

This isn't what I had planned for when I came back home. Ash and I had been looking forward to getting an apartment together. I never wanted this responsibility, and every part of me was telling me I would screw it up.

But Macy had never asked me for anything. How could I refuse her? Especially now.

"Tell me what is going on, and I will move back to help you finish school."

She bit her lip, unsure. After a lifetime her shoulders tensed up. I watched her eyes grow harder and could tell she was steeling herself.

"I can't go to Dad's because I am gay."

I thought a statement like that would shock me. But it felt like a thousand pieces falling into place.

All those arguments about religion. Mom trying to soften my dad towards gay rights and talking about how the rules had to evolve for a changing world. Insisting it wasn't a decision you choose.

All those rumors about Macy my last year of school, not believing them because the Macy I knew was so shy and tight-lipped at home.

My mom knew. She saw ahead and knew what Macy had in store for her. Those fights had been the last straw for their marriage. Mom had chosen Macy and given her a life without my dad and his judgment.

I had never loved my mom more than I did at that moment. I also hated her for not letting me in and preparing me.

"Did you tell Mom?" I asked quietly.

Macy looked confused, thinking I was going to try to tell her she was mistaken about herself and try to lead her to the light.

"Yeah. I came out to her last year. But Dad doesn't know. And I can't hide it while living with him. He will make me hate that part of who I am, and I am barely brave enough to accept it myself."

Macy looked so scared and unsure of herself. I never wanted her to feel that way towards me. I took her hand,

"Okay. I will move back in."

"You're okay with it?"

I closed my eyes, wishing I had seen the signs. I searched my heart, looking for feelings of disgust or anger. Those emotions never came, I was so at peace. It was like the universe was bringing her full circle, and I felt blessed to be a part of it.

I held her hands gently, "I'm okay with it. I love you, every single piece."

*

CJ stood at the fringe of the crowd, consistently sobbing but secure in his isolation. I wanted to go to him and try to comfort him. I wanted to have him hug me back and tell me everything was going to be okay. But he looked more destroyed than I was even allowing myself to feel at the moment.

I held hands with Macy as our dad sat woodenly behind us. People had shaken our hands, hugged us, and told us over and over how sorry they were. It was all wrong. My dad wasn't receiving the grief or even the counsel.

I was too young to have to do this on my own, to have to try to guide Macy through it all. That seemed to be the path my life was veering into.

I thought my dad would be disappointed when I told him that I planned to move into Mom's old house with Macy. But he just seemed relieved and asked me to call him if I ever needed money. So here I was, attending my mom's funeral and having to raise my little sister at only 21 years old.

I looked around at the crowd that had gathered to say goodbye to my mom and wondered who she was to all of these strangers. A friend, a co-worker, maybe even an unrequited crush? I squinted my eyes as I saw flickers behind a few people.

I stared for a full minute before realizing they seemed like pieces of shadows clinging onto living souls. I slammed my eyes shut, imagining my consciousness as a quilt and trying desperately to patch up the broken seams. My hands went cold, and my injured wrist went completely numb in fear.

When I opened my eyes again, the sun was back, and the ceremony was over. I barely hugged Macy goodbye, and she left as quickly as possible with Britney. I ran to my car, to the only person I wanted to be with right now.

"We had the service today," I told Terry, waiting to see a reaction cross her face.

She and my mom had been the closest. I knew it would be the hardest thing for her to hear when she woke up. Not only was our mom gone but she wasn't going to get a chance to send her off.

"I feel like I did a terrible job of setting it up. Hosting. Everything. I had to speak, and last night when I was finishing my eulogy, I was stumped. I kept trying to think of some advice she had given me or a story to share. But I was actually trying to search your memories because you would have known exactly what to say," my voice caught in my throat.

I leaned over our clasped hands, sobbing.

"How can I do this without you? I need you, Terry. I need you to wake up and take care of us like you always do. Playing the peacemaker and making everything look so effortless. You would know exactly what to say to make everyone feel a little better. You would know how to help Macy get through this. You would know which stories to tell to make everyone feel closer to her and able to say goodbye."

My sobs stumbled over each other, scrambling to get out.

"I don't deserve to be the one to say goodbye to her, to be the one who everyone comforts. I deserved this pain. But you didn't."

Finally, I gave in and crawled into the bed next to my sister. Everything inside of me wanted her to put her arms around me and brush my hair back. To share in this pain that was bigger than my body. I just wanted my sister back.

*

"Okay, so let's figure this out. The house is paid for, right? But there is still groceries, bills, and land taxes. How are you planning on paying for everything?" Ash asked.

Planning made her feel safe and honestly, it was incredible to have someone shouldering this responsibility with me in even the smallest way.

"My dad is going to help out some, but it won't be enough. I found some bill schedules on my mom's desk that will give me some idea of what I am in for."

"What about... That night you had some fantastic news. I feel like an asshole for wanting to be excited about that despite this God-awful situation."

I laughed bitterly, thinking back to the exciting news that I had withheld from my mom because it was Terry's night. I went to school for creative writing and had the intention of someday working as a teacher in a high school.

But my real love was writing novels. I had been working on a manuscript since I was 17 and last year, I finally finished it. An agent contacted me after I published the first chapter in a writer's group and everything had moved so quickly.

My book was set to be released next summer.

"Ash, my book... It's about death. It's a child dying and looking for his mother in the afterlife. Now... I can't think about it yet. I kept this from my mom. This was the greatest thing to ever happen to me, and I refused to tell her because I was throwing a fit. Now I will never get the chance," I sobbed, leaning into her and covering my face.

She rubbed my back, not trying to make me feel better and just being there.

There are some moments in life when you truly don't get a second chance. I had done this to myself, now I was completely lost in who I was and what my future held.

*

As I pulled up to my mother's house, I realized that I was dreading this moment with everything I had inside of me.

I had avoided staying here since moving out when I was 16. I refused to go alone and hated being in a room by myself. Over the years I assumed it was because being there would remind me of everything I had left behind. It would bring back the memories of being with my mom and when my parents were together.

But as I sat in my car and stared up at the bay windows from the living room, I grasped that it was much more than that.

The house was dull white with yellow trimmings, an expansive yard that wrapped around the house, and had huge windows that seemed to soak in the sun no matter which room you were in. But there was something darker here, something not everyone could feel.

Something that wasn't obvious from the outside. This house terrified me, and I had completely forgotten just how much.

I wondered how a person forgot something like that. A fear that felt as solid as a hand pressing against your throat. I screamed as a knock rapped on the window next to my head.

Macy's face popped into view; her eyes confused.

"Are you okay? I didn't mean to scare you," she shouted, projecting through the glass.

I put my hand on my chest, trying to get my breathing under control. She motioned to the door with an amused look.

"Then come on."

Taking a deep breath, I opened the door and followed her up the driveway. For the first time since the funeral, I looked around me, waiting to see the dark people hanging out in my mom's yard. If those lost souls would be anywhere, I knew they would find me here.

A part of me knew that my grief had helped me hold onto whatever was left of the veil I had carried with me. But being here, I could feel it slipping away with every step I took into this house and my past.

As I unlocked the door and stepped into the living room, I saw ghosts were the least of my problems right now.

70

One of the windows in the hallway had been broken from the outside and the cold morning air was making the curtains flap like crazy. Dirty footprints started there and led us into my mom's room off of the living room. When I pushed the door inward my breath caught in my throat and my vision blurred.

"What the hell," Macy sobbed, walking into the room and slowly turning in a circle.

Every dresser was upturned, the papers from her desk had been strewn about and ripped. Her blankets were ripped off the bed, and the mattress was thrown against the wall. Even the photos had been thrown, showering the thick carpet with glass.

My mother's books were trampled on, her prized CD collection was on the floor instead of alphabetized, her memories torn apart before we even had a chance to say goodbye. Macy strode out of the room and headed downstairs to where our bedrooms were.

Her bedroom was the first one when you got to the end of the stairs. It was untouched, the same with mine, which was across from the laundry room.

Terry's bedroom was off of the den towards the back of the house. It was even worse than our mom's room. The mattress cut open, and the knick-knacks that were around her room were smashed against the wall, leaving jagged dents in the paint and plaster.

"Why?" Macy cried.

I felt her surprise and hurt so vividly that it made my stomach cramp and my vision swim. This was hard enough. Going through their rooms would have been impossibly painful. Having them destroyed was almost too much to bear.

"I don't get it, is anything missing?" I asked, reaching for my phone to call the police.

"Not that I can tell, it's just ruined," she turned to me, her cheeks wet.

"Okay, I'm calling the police. And Dad, he will know how to get the window fixed and an alarm system installed."

"Who would do this?" Macy asked, turning back to Terry's room.

I shuddered as the car from that night popped into my head. The dirty truck and the man behind the wheel who had run us off the road. That felt personal, this was vengeful.

Fear filled my chest as I became aware he could still be in the house. As I called the police, I walked over to Terry's closet and grabbed her bat from her softball days.

That man had destroyed our lives twice now. If he was still here, I was going to make the third time a lot harder. Macy looked at the bat in my hand and came to the same realization. She stood behind me as we waited quietly for the police to arrive.

*

I have been grocery shopping for myself since I was 16. When I moved in with my dad, I was in charge of keeping the kitchen running. It was something I never minded, and I actually looked forward to it.

We loved trying new recipes, and I felt like such an adult being in charge of cooking. I loved finding coupons and knew our lives inside and out. Looking through these aisles, I was faced with the realization that I might have known my dad and our life then, but I stopped knowing Macy.

I didn't know what cereal she ate. I didn't know if she hated peas or loved sweet potatoes. I realized I had never asked what her favorite food was. I was a shitty sister and knew that nothing.

Buying her Skittles and meatloaf wouldn't make up for how I had discarded everyone. I blindly went through the aisles until my basket was full then headed to the checkout stand in a haze.

"Duct tape. Spam. Zip ties. Are you planning on kidnapping someone and forcing them to live on the meat of Satan?" the cashier asked.

Startled I looked up and recognized Holden, a guy I had gone to high school with. I looked down at my haul for the first time and blushed, seeing the super absorbent tampons and vegan chicken nuggets. I knew we wouldn't eat half of this food but had gone too far to put anything back without looking like a jackass.

"No kidnapping planned," I forced out.

He smiled, and I remembered that he had been friends with my high school boyfriend, Ken. He had always made me laugh in class.

"Then someone really made you mad? Your mom maybe? I haven't seen her in here in a while. She usually stocks up on People and chocolate bars after work."

I bit my lip, struggling to breathe once again.

"Actually, my mom passed away last week."

Holden's eyes looked like they were going to pop out of his head, something that would have made me laugh under different circumstances.

"I am so sorry Claire. I had no idea."

I shrugged, putting the bagged groceries into my cart.

"No, seriously. How is everyone taking it? Are you back home with Terry?"

Tears falling freely now, I shook my head.

"Terry is in a coma. We were in an accident. I am living at their house to take care of Macy. This is all for her, I am trying to grocery shop for her," I said, sobs shaking my shoulders.

I was so thankful that I had decided to come on a Wednesday afternoon when the store was so empty. Holden came around the checkout stand and suddenly engulfed me in an embrace. I tried to stiffen but eventually, let him hold me.

I melted into his arms and just cried out everything I had been holding in. I felt so inadequate for what laid ahead and had to be strong for my family. Something about Holden told me that it was okay to be this out of control, that he would be there without judging.

I felt comfort and peace radiating from him. After collecting myself, Holden took a break to help me load the groceries into my trunk.

"I am sorry, I didn't mean to lose it like that," I said, trying to gather my hair up out of my face where it had stuck to tears and snot.

Holden smiled gently, "Please don't apologize. I think you needed to break down."

I shrugged, wanting to change the subject.

"How long are you staying? Have you seen anyone else from school?" Holden asked, saving me from an awkward transition.

"Um, I am actually moving back to stay. I went to university with Ashley, and we planned on living together but... Things changed. I haven't seen anyone else. I don't even know who else stayed."

"Marci, Eliza, Shawn... Ken. Ken stayed and works at the hardware store now with his dad."

I blew a sigh out, thankful once again I had chosen to lose it in a grocery store instead of trying to shop for nails. Hearing that Ken was still here brought up feelings I thought I had shed along with my graduation gown from high school.

"Well. Thank you. Maybe we will run into each other again?" I said, opening my car door.

"Definitely. Hopefully within the next week so that Macy doesn't have to actually eat any of that crap you bought."

I laughed, surprising myself.

"Sounds good."

He squeezed my shoulder quickly and headed back to the store.

*

I have been protective of my little sister since the day she was born. Some of my earliest memories are of holding her in my arms that barely seemed long enough and pulling her close to my chest.

But I have never felt it more than I did here in this house. She seemed completely at ease here, close to memories of my mom and a childhood she loved. But all I could remember was always feeling on edge. One memory stood out more than others.

In the summertime my sisters and I loved sleeping in the same room, talking until morning and dreaming about who we would be years from now. One of those nights while my sister snoozed next to me, I awoke terrified.

I hadn't been dreaming of anything terrible, but I knew something was in the room. My eyes were drawn to a corner of the room where I had three cupboards built into the wall for books.

None were darker than the others, but the top one filled me with more fear than I thought possible. I could see nothing. But I knew with complete certainty that something was there.

It was playing hide and seek against your will, knowing you weren't alone and that something could jump out at you at any moment. I didn't know if whatever was there was dangerous. The unknown was the worst part.

I stayed awake for hours, looking in that direction and feeling myself fade with the coming morning, and putting my arm over my sister's chest so that she couldn't be touched by the pain in the room. Sleeping in this house was impossible.

Not only was it silent in a way that only a house in a small town can be, but it also creaked every time the wind blew. My room was still decorated like it had been when I was 16 and left.

Emo posters on the wall, drawings of space and poems from English class on my window sill, a bookshelf absolutely stuffed with novels that I knew were dog-eared in the best way. I loved this room, but I hated that girl. I felt suffocated by my past self and my selfishness as a teen. I didn't belong here, and the house knew it.

Giving up on my nights 8 hours I swung my legs out of bed and headed to the hallway to go upstairs for a drink.

As I entered the hall, I felt like I was walking into a wall of steam. Every hair on my arms stood up, and my chest was heavy. The air around me seemed to shimmer, and I was suddenly hit with an overwhelming sense of déjà vu.

I remembered standing in this exact spot when I was 6, where the concrete floor met the carpeted stairs. It was sunny, and I was heading outside to play when I was caught in the kind of steam that filled up the bathroom after a hot shower.

I had looked up, and a little boy with curly red hair was sitting on the top step. He was smiling and looked like he wanted to play. Something inside of me whispered that he couldn't be real. He didn't live here, and maybe he wasn't really here after all.

But I had grinned back, and he sent a small red ball down the stairs. I watched it intently, wondering if my hands would pass through it if I bent down to touch it. As it hit the floor, it bumped my toes, and I felt a breath of bouncy rubber.

I looked up at him.

"My name's Claire."

"Rusty. My names Rusty. Do you want to play?" he asked.

The memory slipped away, leaving me in the cold hallway. I closed my eyes, suddenly terrified. I remembered Rusty always seeming like he was made of light. Like he was always on the verge of shimmering out of my sight. I understood that the people I saw in the hospital the night my mom died had been composed of the exact same shade of rays.

Maybe Rusty had been real all along. Maybe it was my perception that was flawed. I slowly opened my eyes and had to swallow a scream.

Rusty was sitting on the top step, an unsure look on his face. His eyes had dark circles under them, and he was clutching his red ball to his chest.

"You're back," he said, his voice filling me with a million memories of swings and popsicles.

"I'm back," I whispered.

He stared at me before nodding, "You can see it all."

I swallowed, realizing my mom had been right along. My gift had been there every single day of my childhood. But now I was back, and I was naked before the truth.

"Yes. I see it all now."

Chapter Eight

Claire

"You are way too excited about this," I told Ash as I laid a blanket on the ground.

She began to make a circle out of candles and lit them one by one.

"Claire. You have no idea how long I have been waiting for this day."

I rolled my eyes. Ash was the only person I had ever talked about my family's gifts. She accepted it without question. Okay, maybe not without questions. There were a million of questions.

But the belief had always been there. She didn't get why I would push away the possibility of being special and was always trying to analyze me for psychic tendencies.

When I confided in her what had happened at the hospital and about seeing Rusty again, she had literally squealed on the phone and hurried over.

"Did you tell Macy yet?" she asked.

"No! And you can't either. I know the first thing she would want to do is contact Mom and I don't want her to be disappointed if it doesn't work."

"Isn't that the first thing you thought of?" Ash asked, giving me a raised eyebrow.

I twisted my hands together, "Well, yeah. But it's different. I have a lot to apologize for. I don't want Macy to see that and hate me even more."

She crossed the room to squeeze my shoulder, "Macy doesn't hate you. You guys just need some time to get to know each other again and heal. It's no one fault."

I stayed quiet but disagreed. It was my fault. I had so much to make up for. I needed my mom, I needed to apologize and to ask her to help me move forward.

77

"Also, if I know Macy at all I can say that you really can't win right now. She will be upset if you don't include her and she doesn't get a chance to say goodbye. Or, she will be upset if it doesn't work and she got her hopes up."

I sighed, "Then what? What do I do?"

"Does her not being here feel right?" Ash asked.

I nodded, and she nodded back, the decision made. We sat in the circle of candles, something I wanted to blush over because this was like a scene out of the Craft. If my dad could only see me now. As the silence stretched on, I saw that Ash was waiting for me to kick this thing off.

I bit my lip and shrugged, "I'm not really sure how to start this. Every other time it happened they seemed to find me. I didn't do anything that I am aware of to force it."

"Maybe we try to talk to her?" she suggested.

I took a deep breath and closed my eyes, trying to focus all my energy on connecting with the energy around me.

"I am here, ready to receive any sign you want to give me. I am here Mom, waiting for you."

"That was good. You're a natural," Ash said. I opened one eye to see her nodding enthusiastically.

"Ash, this is serious. Quit complimenting me. I feel like one of those dial a psychic, and you are one of my groupies spending all of your money $1 at a time."

"Take it all. Just let me grab my wallet."

I laughed but smacked her knee, "Concentrate."

After sitting in silence for over an hour, I let out a big breath, way more disappointed than I wanted to be.

Ash leaned forward to hold my hand, "This was our first try. Don't be discouraged. The more you use it, the easier it will get."

I tried to appear unfazed, but I knew what had happened.

My mom was angry with me. She blamed me for the accident. She didn't want to talk to me, to show me a sign. I didn't deserve her forgiveness.

*

The nurse coming out of Terry's room smiled and motioned me inside.

"She has a visitor already, but go ahead."

CJ was sitting next to her, a CD player on his lap and earphones covering Terry's ears. I crossed the room to give him a small hug.

"How are you?" he asked, rubbing my back and then pulling a chair over so that I could sit next to him.

I shrugged, "I feel completely… numb. In limbo. I'm trying to focus on doing what Macy needs me to do."

CJ squeezed my shoulder, "I'm proud of you. For stepping up."

I knew that he thought I should have stepped up years ago. I was pretty terrible to Terry at times during our childhood and CJ was her best friend. He could hate me a little bit on her account because she was never as hard on me as she should have been.

He patted my hand, satisfied with how ashamed I was.

"What is she listening to?" I asked, motioning to the CD player.

"Mixes we made in college. I read that extra stimulation could jolt her memory. Maybe even get a big enough response to wake her up. I think of it as an exercise for her brain."

I leaned forward and squeezed her hand, wanting her to squeeze back. We sat in silence for a few minutes then CJ looked at his phone.

"Time for work," he told me, standing up and carefully removing Terry's headphones.

He wrapped them around the CD player than casually leaned down and kissed Terry's lips. I looked at him in shock, but he only hugged me and then left me alone with my thoughts. I couldn't help but giggle a little bit.

CJ was gorgeous, he always had been. Macy and I had a huge crush on him in elementary school. He had curly black hair that always wrapped around his ears no matter how many haircuts he had. He had the darkest eyes I have ever seen and the most contagious smile.

We got over our crushes because we were also sure boys had cooties. But he and Terry never seemed to make up their minds about who they were to each other.

When I was in middle school, I remembered a summer where they started kissing out of nowhere. I would see them from the kitchen window, reading each other sections of novels and stealing kisses in the clubhouse. They held hands while walking home and he called her every single evening to say goodnight.

Then just as suddenly, they weren't kissing anymore. There was no fight. They still saw each other multiple times a week. He still looked at her the same way. He still called her every single night.

Yet, CJ started dating another girl that year in school, and Terry supported him. I never doubted that he somehow was Terry's and that she was his. But it was more complicated than I could ever understand. Whenever I asked her about him, she told me that he was her best friend and she loved him.

But it was more than that. Maybe it was more than she would ever be able to put into words herself.

He had been her constant for the past twenty years. He was a part of our family. I leaned towards Terry's ear and laid my head on her shoulder.

"Wake up Ter. I think he's ready to do this with you. I wish you were willing to do this with him. He loves you so much, Ter. It's worth waking up for."

*

The darkness and silence of the house were suffocating. At night I went through the motions of getting ready for bed. I took a shower, brushed my teeth, got into my nightshirt, and laid in bed. I closed my eyes then I laid here until I couldn't breathe.

Instead, I ended up wandering around the house and tried to make myself part of it again. For the third night in a row, I threw the blanket off of my legs and headed out into the hallway.

80

As I rounded the corner, I heard muffled sobbing coming from Macy's room. I knocked quietly then pushed the door open. She rolled over to face me, her cheeks puffy and tear-stained.

My heart twisted until I thought it would crack in half. I kneeled next to her bed and wrapped my arm around her.

"Shhh, Shhh," I shushed her quietly.

"Why haven't you cried?" Macy whispered.

I sat back on my heels, "What?"

She sat up, her eyes angry and accusing. This is what Macy always did. When she was hurt, she struck out. She wanted to push everyone away so that they had to fight tooth and nail to find their way to her again.

"Why haven't you cried? At the funeral, while we cleaned up, it's been weeks. Why are you okay? Did you not care that mom died? Do you not care that Terry's body is broken and that she might die too?" she sobbed, pushing my hand away.

"Macy, that's a shitty thing to ask," my voice was thick coming out of my throat.

She shrugged, "It's true. You don't care."

I dropped my head, "Just because I haven't cried in front of you doesn't mean it hasn't happened."

"Why would you hide that from me?" she asked, crossing her arms.

I looked up at her, frustrated, "Because that's how this goes, Macy. You asked me to take care of you. That means keeping it together so that you can lose it. So, I can help you put things back together."

As the words left my mouth, I thought back to Terry and those years after the divorce. She had never cried. She had fed us, cleaned the house, and got Mom back on her feet. She comforted us over and over. She hadn't lost it, or at least that's what I always assumed.

But now, I knew without a doubt that she had cried a million times. That she had cried all by herself.

I wished more than anything I could have changed that and been able to hold her. To make her feel safe instead of making her feel like she had to keep everyone together.

"This is what Terry would have done, Terry would have been strong," I said, my voice breaking and my eyes filling with tears regardless.

Macy's eyes swelled, and my face reflected back to me in her tears. She scooted back in her bed and pulled back the blanket so that I could sit next to her. I crawled in and gripped her in a hug.

We cried, holding onto each other until the sun started peeking through Macy's pink curtains. Only then were we both able to fall fully to sleep for the first time in almost a month.

*

Ash's easy conversation with Macy made me jealous, I couldn't help but stare as they tried to create an edible dinner out of the groceries I had bought.

My phone ringing saved me from torturing myself with their relationship. I didn't recognize the number but answered anyway.

"Hello?"

"Hi, please don't think I am a stalker or anything. I got your number from Facebook."

My eyebrows furrowed as I tried to place the familiar voice, "Who is this?"

"Oh my God, this phone call couldn't get any more awkward. I should have just texted."

I laughed, "I forgive you."

"It's Holden. I still feel like an ass for bringing up... Your recent loss and wanted to know if I could make it up to you."

"By doing what?"

"Bringing you dinner? I made a huge pan of chicken parmesan and would love to share it with you and Macy."

"Well... Ash is here too."

"I'm sure she eats. Unless she doesn't, in which case it doesn't matter."

I put my hand on my phone and grabbed Ash's arm so that she would turn around, "It's Holden from the grocery store. High school Holden? He wants to bring us dinner. What do you think?"

"Thank God," said Macy, immediately dumping whatever she had been trying to sauté into the sink.

"Let's do it," Ash said, agreeing with a grin I definitely didn't like.

"Okay. Do you need my address? I don't know how thorough Facebook is."

He paused, embarrassed, "Actually no. I don't need it. I remember the house from high school when Ken and I used to drop you off after school."

After hanging up, Ash gave me a silly grin.

"Is this weird?" I asked.

She shrugged, "It doesn't have to be. We used to hang out all the time."

"Yeah, but that was with Ken. Who I guess still lives here, but I haven't run into him at all."

She narrowed her eyes at me, "Do you want to run into him?"

I blushed, "I don't know, Ash. I loved him, you know I did. He was the only guy I have ever loved. It's hard to know he is here and not be curious about what he is up to."

"I get that. But I also get that he was always a dickhead who doesn't even deserve your curiosity."

"Who's a dickhead?" said Macy, suddenly interested in the conversation.

"Ken. Do you remember him?" Ash asked.

"Sure. Claire's high school boyfriend. The whole thing was very dramatic. He cheated, didn't he? Isn't that why you dumped him?"

If possible, I blushed even deeper.

"Yes and no. He cheated..." "

A lot," interrupted Ash.

"Yes, a lot. And I was an ass who kept taking him back. Then, right after graduation, he dumped me."

Macy shook her head, "Ouch."

As the doorbell rang, I stood and glared at them.

"Yes, ouch. It was hard. I think I am over it. Please don't talk about it around Holden. He was a friend from school, and it's nice to have people around us that care."

Ash put her hands up in surrender, but I knew this wasn't the end of the Ken conversation.

Once I let Holden in it was easy to remember why we had always gotten along. He was funny in a very unassuming way and seemed to be at home wherever he was. He remembered Macy and asked about her life, which touched me for some reason.

Ash and he had a quick rapport, and before we knew it, the delicious dinner he had made was eaten, and we had been sitting around the table talking for hours.

Holden had been working in the grocery store since high school and recently had decided he was going to be a lifer. It was a family business, and his dad was nearing retirement. It was a good job and would keep him close to his family. He talked about his life comfortably and wanted to know more about our life before we came back home.

Macy looked down at her phone screen, and her eyes widened, "Oh man. I need to go to bed. It's already 11, and I have school tomorrow."

Holden looked surprised.

"Of course. Well, I guess I better head out then."

I stood and headed to the stove.

"Let me wash your pan for you."

He shook his head.

"Take your time. I'll get it next time."

After saying goodbye, he let himself out.

"Claire! Why weren't you dating him in school? He is a fox."

"Psh, please. He was Ken's best friend."

Ash leaned back in her chair.

"Honestly, it's hard for me to even picture even though I was there. He is the complete opposite of Ken. How in the world does that friendship even begin?"

I shrugged, "I honestly can't remember either. Holden was kind of outshined by Ken. He was his quiet sidekick, and he didn't want to be in the limelight."

"Well, I will tell you one thing. There will be a next time. That was smooth, him leaving his pan so that he could see you again."

Macy giggled as I shook my head.

"No, he just didn't want to overstay his welcome."

"Did you feel like he was?" Macy asked with a sly arched eyebrow.

I smiled back despite myself.

"No. He's nice, and it was all very friendly."

Ash wiggled her eyebrows at Macy.

"For now."

I ignored their giggling as I busied myself with the dishes. Seeing Holden had definitely been nice, but all it seemed to do was bring back a million unresolved feelings from my 17-year-old self.

Had Holden told Ken I was here? When would I see him again? Did I want to see Ken again?

Despite Ash's warning, I knew the answer was yes. It was hard to leave the idea of your first love behind, especially during a time where something sweet from the past felt like it would heal so much in your heart.

*

The bills were piling up, and I wanted to pay them. I knew that my mom had left money that would cover at least the next three months' worth of utilities and electricity.

However, I had no idea how to access it. Her bank account information had been left with us, but when I tried to access her account from my laptop, the bank didn't recognize my computer and needed a security code.

Macy suggested using my mom's computer so that the connection was secure. I found her laptop in her room, where we left it the week after the funeral. Staying in there was too much with her scent all around, so I took it back to my bedroom.

Opening the laptop, I saw that her screensaver was a photo of the three of us girls, my favorite photo from my childhood. We were on our back-porch shucking corn and had posed with our bowl of fresh corn on top of our heads.

All of us were filthy, and I remembered that we had just come from playing in our kiddie pool and then doing gymnastics on the lawn. My damp knees were covered in grass and Macy had a dirt smear around her whole mouth like a clown. We were happy, we were together, and life was perfect.

Swallowing the lump in my throat, I pulled up her browser.

As I started to type in her bank web address her previous history began to fill itself in with the help of Google. Domestic Violence Laws in Washington. Domestic Violence Family Law. WomensLaw.org.

"Macy? Come here," I called, leaning towards my open door.

"What's up?" she said, leaning against my doorjamb.

"Look at this," I said, turning the screen so that she could see it. She leaned down and read the screen.

"That is weird. Was Mom searching for this info?"

I shrugged.

"Or maybe Terry borrowed her computer?"

"No. Terry has her own. Who is Cathy and Gina Shaw? She searched for them a ton of times."

"I don't know. Didn't she mention them to you? Or this guy, Lucas? This is all she looked at the last month."

Macy furrowed her eyebrows.

"No. But I didn't exactly ask for the details of their days. Mom worked with old people that were always dying and Terry would never discuss her patients."

"Maybe they were helping one of her patients together? She seemed worried about it. This is a lot of Googling about one family."

Macy gave me a tense look.

"Who said she was worried? Maybe it was research for Terry."

As she left to go back to her homework, I couldn't shake the heavy feeling settling over me. Macy might not want to think that there was anyone in the world that would want to hurt Mom.

Yet, we couldn't deny that a man had run us off the road that night. Not only that, but their rooms were destroyed when we came back to the house. Cathy and Gina must be connected to whatever happened. The police never gave us any information or told us what steps to take to protect ourselves.

I was helpless with only half a story but knew that I was at fault for not asking sooner. This is what I needed to do to make up for it all. I needed to find out what happened so that I could protect Macy.

*

The smallest things gave me anxiety in this house. Being alone, dark corners, forgetting to set the alarm system even during the day.

But cleaning seemed to be the worst. I hated the white noise of washing dishes or vacuuming. The banging around didn't seem to drown anything out. It was too loud. It gave other noises permission to sneak in while my back was turned.

I was convinced that the only thing that was safe was silence.

I pushed the vacuum through the living room upstairs and tried to keep my back to the wall so I could see the whole room. This room probably got the least use out of the entire house.

The front door led into the living room then broke off into the dining room and kitchen. Through the living room was a sunroom with cupboards and bookshelves with French glass doors. If we were upstairs, we were either eating or reading by the natural light in the sunroom.

When we wanted to watch a movie, we went downstairs to the living room outside of our rooms where our old box set and shelves of DVD's and VHS's still sat from our childhood. Despite the disuse, this room always got dusty so quickly. I ran the vacuum through the room, and as I pivoted to get a corner, I became aware of movement from the corner of my eye.

I froze but didn't turn off the vacuum. From my peripheral vision, I watched the corner to my right darken. But it wasn't only a solid shadow. It was a shadow that seemed to have shoulders and arms that slightly stuck out. As I stood frozen in terror the shadow took a step forward, the darkness coming with it.

The back door slammed shut, and Macy's footsteps announced her arrival from school. I turned, looking to the corner. The room was sunny once again.

I turned off the vacuum and sat right on the ground, trying to control my racing heart. Macy came in and dropped the mail on the coffee table.

"You okay?"

I shook my head, pretending like I was finished and coiling the cord back up. I wanted to tell Macy what had happened, these shadows were becoming more and more regular.

But acknowledging them felt like the worst mistake that I could make. Acknowledging them felt like it would give them more power.

*

I had been avoiding Ash for the past two days because she always could see right through me. In high school, she knew immediately if Ken and I had been arguing. Not only could she guess the reason why, but she would scold me for hours for not standing up for him.

But she didn't understand. No one noticed me in high school. Terry had been a social butterfly, and it was hard being her shy sister. I was always an add on to her stories without any real sparkle of my own.

So, when Ken asked me out, it was like a dream come true. He was more than just cute; his sky-blue eyes and jet-black hair made me the envy of all the other girls in our grade. He was the first person who ever told me I was beautiful and when it was just him and me, I was so sure of us. He had been my first for so many things, my first kiss, my first time getting to first and second base.

He took me to my first high school dance and listened to me when I vented about moving to my dad's house. He was mine when I was dealing with feeling like I didn't belong to anyone. He would always be the first to me.

So, when I bumped into Ken at the gas station two days before it had felt like destiny revisiting me right when I needed him most. He looked exactly the same and went for a hug immediately, looking stunned by me in the best way.

He told me I looked great and invited me out for dinner that weekend. I had accepted automatically and was really excited.

I didn't want Ash to know yet. I didn't want her to have a chance to crap on this before I knew exactly where this was heading.

Also, it had only been a month since my mom's death. I didn't know if Macy or Ash would understand me needing some kind of distraction.

He was the best kind. If I was honest with myself, I had held onto Ken throughout college. I had dated two other guys but never entirely gave them my heart. My heart was still in Spokane.

At 6:30 I met Ken at the same Olive Garden where we had our first date. I was wearing a purple dress and so nervous I felt 16 again. After waiting for about 15 minutes Ken breezed in, looking casual in khaki shorts and a button up.

"Hey, sorry I'm late. I was getting my oil changed."

I waved his apology away, "I just got here."

After getting settled at our table, I started to feel the years between us as the silence stretched on.

"I hear that you are working at the hardware store?" I started, hiding my sweaty hands under my thighs.

"From who?" he asked, giving me a defensive eyebrow.

I blushed, remembering that he had talked more than anyone about leaving Spokane someday for much greener pastures. He had always felt like a big fish in a small pond.

"From around. I think it's great. Didn't your dad work in that area?"

Ken smiled finally, "Yeah. It kind of fell into my lap after graduation. I worked my way up, and now I am the manager. I'm going to own it one day."

"Wow. Good for you."

He smirked, beginning to pursue his menu. The fact that he didn't ask what I was up to did not escape me.

"Well, I just graduated from Central with a degree in Creative Writing."

Ken snorted, "Sounds like that will make you great money."

I flushed. I had talked about my dreams of writing often as a teenager. He had listened to a thousand rants about me wanting to be an author and to communicate with people through the written word. It was never about money; it had never been.

Had he forgotten how he had once seemed to support that?

"Maybe someday. For right now I am focusing on taking care of Macy and getting her through high school."

Concern filled his eyes, and he leaned forward, covering my hand with his.

"That's right. I heard about your mom. I am so sorry."

"Thank you."

"But what about Terry? Isn't she the oldest? You shouldn't have to take care of Macy when someone else can do it."

My stomach dropped as I looked at him for the first time. Really looked at him and what made him up as a person. I took a deep breath and let myself really feel how he had made me feel all these years.

I loved him, sure. But maybe your first love didn't always deserve those innocent feelings. Because you have never been hurt it's harder to see their flaws. You accept the worst from them.

"I don't feel like I had to. It's the right thing to do," I said shortly, picking up my own menu.

He sighed like I was dramatic and suddenly looked me up and down. I wished I had worn a sweater over my dress.

"You really do look great. College looks good on you."

"Well, it shouldn't anymore. I graduated. With honors."

He kept leering at me.

"So, did you get everything you wanted out of the experience?" he asked, leaning in so that he could speak softly.

"Like?"

"Sex?"

I gasped, and he laughed so loudly the couple at the next table looked over at him.

"I knew it. You kept your virginity that whole time. I knew this was what this was about. You saved it, and you came back for me."

I blushed again, this time in anger.

Four years ago, Ken had pressured me to have sex with him even though I insisted I wasn't ready. After graduation, he told me that if I didn't then, he would never really know if I loved him. He wanted my first time to belong to him and him only.

I went as far as getting undressed before I chickened out. He dumped me, for the millionth time, while I was still naked on his bed. Then he left me at his house all alone, and I had to walk the six blocks to my house in the dark.

I was heartbroken. I spent the first six months of college crying in my room and missing so many fun rites of passage.

"Actually, I didn't," I said, leaning back in my chair and watching his face.

He stopped laughing, and some color came into his cheeks.

"No?"

"No. I got exactly what I wanted. From college guys, with experience. I came back because I graduated and wanted to be with my family. You never left, maybe it was you who was waiting."

Ken bit his lip, a tell from long ago that he was about to lose his temper.

"Being a whore is nothing to brag about."

This time I laughed, shocking him. I thought back to our relationship and how many nights I was alone while he avoided my calls. I remembered the decisions I made after healing from what he did to me.

"Goodbye, Ken," I said, for the first time really mean it.

I grabbed my purse and headed out to my car. I thought I might feel ruined by him once again. However, as I sat in my car, I couldn't help but laugh at myself.

What had I ever seen in him? He hadn't changed, I had.

I was not only seeing Ken for the first time, I saw myself. I saw what I had sought out in him. Acceptance, love, and a warm place that was comfortable when I didn't feel comfortable in my own skin. I had become addicted to him because I never fully had his heart.

Loving Ken when he didn't love me back had destroyed my self-esteem for years. Now that I looked back at him, I couldn't even remember falling in love with him in the first place.

He didn't have a great job and wasn't destined for greatness even back then. He wasn't a good man, and he wasn't really all that good looking. He had told me I was beautiful at a time in my life when I felt like I was nothing.

He pretended to think I was more than that but worked very hard to push me into a small box so that I was always there when he was lonely. He was pathetic, and I was disgusted at my past self for letting him change how I felt about myself.

I was done. He had no power over me anymore. I leaned my head against my seat, thinking of Holden.

He had never said they were friends and had even skirted Ken as a topic. If they weren't friends and he wasn't trying to set us back up, why the sudden reconnection? Was there something there I had never considered?

*

"Hey, I'm going out for a couple of hours," Macy said, poking her head into my bedroom where I was reorganizing my bookshelf with the boxes I brought from my dorm.

Finding a space for my college self and belongings was hard. I didn't know what to throw away, I didn't know what to keep. I was already on edge and just wanted privacy.

"Uh," I stood up and dusted off my hands.

These were the conversations I had been looking forward to the least. I had never grown up in this house as a teenager and my rules at Dad's house could have been completely different.

I didn't know Macy's curfew or what my mom would have been okay with. I wanted to let Macy go her own way but knew my mom would also want her to have some semblance of normalcy.

"It's a Wednesday. Don't you have homework you should be doing? Maybe you could ask your friends to come over here?"

She raised an eyebrow at me, "Why? Do you need to watch me? I'm not a child, Claire."

"I'm not saying you are. I'm just saying, it's 9:30 and a week night. I don't know what Mom's rules were, but that doesn't sound like something she would agree to."

Macy's face turned a light shade of pink, "So now we care what Mom would have wanted?"

My throat tightened, and I couldn't help but blush.

"When it comes to keeping you safe, I have always cared what she wanted," I replied quietly.

"Whatever. I'll be back soon."

She attempted to shut my door, but I jumped forward to grab the knob and pull it open.

"I said no, Macy."

"You're not my boss!" she yelled, her bottom lip beginning to tremble.

I suddenly remembered her crying whenever she didn't get her way. It was her defensive mechanism even back when she was a little girl trying to tell me how to play Barbie's.

"For the next year, I am. Unless you want to go live with Dad."

Her lips thinned in anger, "Are you threatening me? When you know how I feel about that?"

I threw my hands up. Was there any way to win in this situation?

"Macy, I don't know how to make it clear to you that I don't want to be your boss. I never wanted this responsibility, and I agreed because I love you. But you have to meet me halfway here."

"Why? You never cared before. I still can't believe you said yes. I bet you have some calendar hidden, counting down the days until I graduate."

Now I was crying. I was doing my best. Why couldn't she see that?

"Of course not. I am trying to help you. I don't know what Mom's rules were. I'm trying to figure this out as we go along."

"But that's the thing," Macy said, wiping her nose on her sweater.

"What?"

"You could have known. You could have stayed. But you didn't. You left. And I don't know if I can forgive you for pushing Mom away. For being okay with missing me growing up."

I covered my face, sobbing.

"I don't know if I can forgive myself either. But I'm trying to be here now," I said, sitting on my bed.

Macy shook her head and walked away from my door. I thought she would leave anyway, but she only went down the hall back to her room and quietly closed her door.

*

The next morning after we fought, I dreaded seeing Macy, but she had already left by the time I went into the kitchen for coffee. I took a deep breath, also feeling sad that I hadn't told her how sorry I was.

As I grabbed a mug out of the cupboard, I saw a note on the counter.

Claire,
Mom used to put this pad of paper on the fridge during the summer so that we could add requests to the grocery list. I thought this would make shopping easier. I added some things that we usually had for lunch, and you can add whatever you want.
Also, my curfew on school days is 10. On weekends and summertime, it's 11, the same as Terry when she was in high school.

94

I am not allowed to have Britney sleep over and when she is here my door has to be open at all times.

I also was asked to check in close to my curfew in case I need a ride.

Thank you for staying here. I know it's not easy. I know you're trying.

Love you,
Macy

I took a relieved breath, folding the note up and putting it in the pocket of my pajama pants. I looked at the grocery list pad on the fridge. It looked like Macy's favorite dinner was still Filipino chicken, just like when she was little. That reassured me in a way I couldn't describe.

*

When I was growing up in this house, I always felt watched. Especially when I was at my most vulnerable. I would dress with my back to the wall so that I could fully see the room around me. I hated washing my face in the shower.

It was something I thought I had outgrown because the feeling did not seem to follow me to college. But as soon as I was back in this house, in this bathroom, it was all coming back to me.

I was attempting to soak in a bath with a Stephen King novel, an obviously bad choice given the circumstances. I was avoiding washing my hair and putting my head underwater in any way because I was surer than ever that I was being watched.

I took a deep breath, giving up on my book and laying it next to the tub. As I leaned over the side, I looked up at the fogged over mirror. I gasped as I saw a small hand print on the corner of the mirror. I quickly jumped out and self-consciously wrapped myself in a towel.

As I headed to my room the feeling became so intense, I was choking on it. I shoved my door open and saw Rusty sitting on my bed.

95

"Rusty, were you in the bathroom?" I whispered, shutting the door behind me.

I thought he looked tired when I first saw him sitting on the stairs, yet he looked even worse now. Dark purple bruises stained his green eyes. He was chewing on his lips angrily as he avoided my stare.

"No, I just touched the mirror. I needed to talk to you."

"So, you scared me?" I asked.

He smiled so callously that the hair on the back of my neck stood on end. At a loss, I grabbed some clean clothes and went into Terry's room to change.

Once I was decent, I went back to my room. Rusty was looking at the photographs on my desk.

"What did you need to talk to me about? Why are you so angry?"

He spun, his eyes flashing.

"About me being by myself for years. They couldn't see or hear me. You promised to help me, you promised!"

"I promised? When?"

But even as I said it, I was reeling with the memory.

Rusty and I sat out on the back porch. I was reading, and he was looking over my shoulder, struggling with the words. I comprehended for the first time that he was only a little boy and had been ever since I met him.

I asked him why he never had a birthday and he cried. He told me that he would never have another birthday, but he was okay with that as long as he found his mom. He knew that she was alone, and he couldn't leave until he found her.

The idea of being that alone in the world broke my heart into pieces. I promised him that I would always be his friend and that he would find his mom someday.

I sank to the ground, my hands shaking.

"Rusty, I didn't think you were real. I was such a lonely little girl, and part of me figured I had made you up entirely. When I turned 12, I wasn't able to see you anymore."

"Because you didn't want to!" he yelled, his hands balled into small fists.

"That's not true!" I yelled back, knowing it was a lie but unable to admit how much I had deserted him.

When I was 10, Terry had fully received her gift. It caused a lot of problems in my family's marriage. I became a have not so that my dad wouldn't be left alone.

I had forced myself to believe that I had only imagined Rusty. I threw him away.

I covered my face, crying. Rusty slowly walked over to my dresser and ripped open the top drawer. He lifted my jeans to pull out my manuscript, the one recently accepted for publication.

He threw the manuscript in the direction of my lap and left the room, dissipating as he crossed the threshold into the hallway. I flipped through the script, shaking with emotion. I truly understood why this story was always in my head.

I finally saw the book as a repressed memory. The story followed Len and Rusty, two 5-year-old friends during the best summer of their lives. Back then I don't think Rusty shared his death story with me, regardless, it was inside of my head this whole time.

I knew how he died. I knew his story. And I had written it hundreds of miles away. I owed him an ending. I had made him a promise after all.

Chapter Nine

Claire

The mail addressed to Terry had been easy to handle. Most of it had been bills, and I opened them immediately so that we weren't drowning in debt along with everything else.

But her phone ringing was something else entirely. Macy looked at the counter where it had been sitting since, we brought it back from the hospital.

I leaned back, wanting nothing to do with it. If it was Lucy from work, I had no idea what to say. Macy shook her head at me and picked it up.

"Hello? Hi, no this is her sister, Macy... No, she isn't available. No, Terry is actually at the hospital. She's not having surgery; she is in a coma. She was in an accident."

Macy's eyes widened, and after a couple minutes she hung up.

"What was that?" I asked, putting down my magazine as Macy handed the phone to me.

"One of Terry's patients I am guessing."

I opened the phone and read the caller ID.

"Gina, why does that name sound familiar? Should we call the office?"

Macy bit her lip, "It didn't feel like a normal check in call. When she found out that Terry was hurt, she freaked out. She started wailing, saying she wasn't safe and that he had found Terry first."

My hands went icy, and I dropped the phone. My thoughts immediately went to the man on the road that night, the one that had run Terry's car off the road. The man that ended up killing my mom.

I could tell Macy's thoughts were headed in the same direction.

"Do you think it was him?" she asked, her voice cracking and her eyes watering.

I was so angry and helpless. I wanted to do something to help. To hold someone accountable for what had happened to my family. The police treated the whole thing as a hit and run and hadn't contacted us since the hospital.

Something about the name Gina tickled the back of my mind and felt important.

"Has she ever brought up this lady to you?"

Macy shook her head.

"Never. We don't talk about her job at all."

I contemplated looking through her phone but didn't know her password. As I stared at her screen, I suddenly remembered my mom's cryptic Google history. Gina and Cathy Carlton.

"Mac, this is the girl from mom's computer research. Do you know Terry's password? We have to figure out who she is. She could lead us to whoever that guy is."

Macy shook her head no then brightened suddenly.

"There may be a way to find out. Where did you put Terry's keys?"

I grabbed them out of my purse and followed her downstairs to Terry's room.

"This is where Terry works when she is home," Macy sat in her office chair and chose a small key from the key ring.

She unlocked the second drawer of a small filing cabinet next to the desk and pulled out their contents. Six manila folders were in the drawer with highlighters and pens.

"She brings her files home?" I asked, sitting on the bed.

"Only the files that she needs to take notes on. I bet you one is from Gina if the case was really complicated. She and mom were really secretive the last couple of months. I assumed they were dealing with something sad and didn't want me to feel bad about it. Mom was super diligent about keeping me sheltered from the hardest parts of their jobs."

I knew that was absolutely true. Whenever I asked either one of them about how their day was going, they always avoided the question and tried to turn the conversation back to me. It was private, it was what they cared about more than anything.

I had been bitter about it a lot while growing up. It had felt like they cared more about strangers than what was happening right in their family. Until now, I had never understood how their gifts had allowed them to help people in a way no one else could.

I was so proud of them and ashamed of myself at the same time. Macy pulled out Gina's file and handed it to me. As I read, I broke out into goosebumps.

"Terry took daily notes from her sessions. It looks like a couple months ago Ter had a vision while with Gina. It was about an old lady being smothered."

"What?!" Macy sat next to me and read over my shoulder.

"This is different though. Terry's visions were always from the past. Did she see into the future? Why did this scare her so much unless it hadn't happened yet?"

Macy looked at me with her eyebrow crooked, "How do you know how Terry's visions were? You refused to let her talk about it."

I blushed. Macy sighed and laid her head on my shoulder.

"I'm sorry."

I bit the inside of my cheek; it was a hard habit to break. We kept reading. We read how the lady in Terry's visions ended up being Cathy, and how that connected mom to the case. We read about Gina's awful family history and her relationship with Lucas.

The last entry was from the week of the accident when Gina's brother killed himself and Terry thought that he did it because he was planning on killing his mom. I took a deep breath, feeling heady from the rush of information.

"Does this mean that it's over?" Macy asked.

"How could it be? This was dated a week before everything happened. The brother was already dead. Terry let her guard down, and someone ran them off the road then ripped our house apart."

Macy started flipping through the file again.

"Then who is it? Lucas, the ex-fiancé? Terry helped Gina escape from him. She confronted him. He visited her at work and threatened her."

"I think so. He crashed into us and then came here to try to find where Gina is staying."

Macy started crying, and I gently pulled her into a hug, not knowing whether or not she would let me. Macy was stiff but let me pat her back as she sobbed. For a moment I didn't care about the accident or Lucas. I hated myself for being so out of the loop.

If I had been here, maybe I would have been able to save them.

*

"So where is your dad tonight?" Ash asked, putting the potato salad she made next to the hamburgers Holden had barbecued.

"Home. I asked him if he wanted to come over and he got super weird."

Ash gave me a half smile.

"Do you blame him? I mean not only is he not the backyard BBQ kind of dad, but this was also his house with his newly deceased ex-wife."

"No, I get it. I just wish one of them was here. Everything reminds me of my mom and it being a special occasion only makes her being gone harder. This is the first holiday since the accident, even though it's only the 4th of July. It's only been a month since Mom passed away. I feel like Macy needed the stability."

Ash sat at the picnic table and looked over to where Macy and Britney were playing in the pool. They had been taking turns doing cannon balls all afternoon, screaming the whole time. There was no hesitation behind their intimacy, and something inside of me knew it was right for her.

I nodded firmly to myself, thinking of how maybe she needed this normalcy more than our dad being here and her being on guard.

"I bet she's relieved to be done with school for now."

"Yep. She worked so hard that I wasn't even upset when she saw Holden at the grocery store yesterday and invited him over."

Ash laughed, "Okay. If she didn't, who was going to work the grill?"

I laughed with her, "Alright. I may have been more than okay with it. Ulterior motives were involved."

She grinned with raised eyebrows.

"Ulterior motives?"

I blushed but shook my head.

"Not that kind. I was only worried about the beef."

She snorted, and my blushed deepened.

"Shut up Ash. You know what I mean."

Holden turned slightly, hearing us laugh and instinctively smiling. I smiled back at him as he turned back to finish the hamburgers.

"I think it's okay if you like him," she told me, trying to act nonchalant.

"I don't know. But I am so thankful that all of this Ken craziness is over. I was curious about him still. But now I realize that I put him on a pedestal. And now it's over."

She leaned forward to give me a high five.

"Thank the Lord."

"It's not just that though. I have been thinking a lot about my mom and sister's lives, how important their gifts were to them. They didn't date, like at all. I wonder if that's connected. They put everything into helping people and dating can make that complicated. It feels wrong to consider being with someone when they never got that. Especially when it's so close to losing them."

Ash leaned over to hold my hand.

"If I know them at all, I know that they would want you to be happy. They wouldn't want you to be so sad that you stopped living your life. If anything, allowing yourself to be happy sets a good example for Macy. She needs to know that her relationship is okay. That letting someone comfort you is more than okay."

I shook my head but still wasn't entirely sure. As much as I didn't want to admit it, it had been hard to stop thinking about Holden since he came over for dinner.

My attraction to him kept surprising me, I had never given him a second though while we were in school together. I thought about his golden blonde hair and dark blue eyes when I was supposed to be making lunch. I heard his contagious laugh when washing dishes, and craved the easy way he made me smile.

But these feelings were always followed with a sense of guilt and ill timing.

Dinner was simple but good. We talked a lot; Britney was very forthcoming and completely charming. With our meal finished, Ash, Holden, and I settled on the porch to watch the fireworks.

"I will be back by 1," Macy said, leaning down to hug me.

"11," I said easily, smiling at her.

She rolled her eyes but agreed.

"11 it is. Thank you for dinner," Britney said, smiling at me and holding Macy's hand.

I watched them disappear out of the driveway, talking loudly about the fireworks they were going to set off and swinging their clasped hands.

"She's happy, right?" I asked Ash.

Ash grinned, giving me that as her answer. As the fireworks started, I began thinking back to the celebrations we had while I was growing up.

Before my parents divorced, we used to go to my dad's business partners house to watch the firework show. He lived really close to the where they were set off, and nothing blocked the view. The first time I remember actually watching it, I was terrified. They were so close that the boom amazed me.

However, as the sparkles began to fall and fade away, they looked like they would fall directly on us. I pictured them hitting the house and setting it on fire. Setting me on fire. I started crying, and my mom pulled me into her lap and wrapped me in a blanket.

With every new starburst, she told me about the colors, how the fireworks were made and told me stories about them. How the blue explosion wanted to be silver because it was everyone's favorite. She told me about how he went back to firework school with dreams of being in the grand finale. Thinking back, I hadn't been afraid by the end of the night, and I was already looking forward to the firework show next year.

"I'm going to run to the gas station for some beer. This feels like a night for a beer and midnight pizza. Need anything?" Ash asked, grabbing her purse from the table.

"Milk, please. Macy drank the last of it this morning."

She grabbed her keys off the picnic table and headed to her car. As she left, I was extremely aware that Holden and I were alone for the first time. I realized that it didn't make me feel uncomfortable despite how new our rekindled friendship was.

"I went to dinner with Ken," I said, turning to him to see his reaction.

His eyebrows furrowed for a moment before he forced a smile, "How did that go?"

"He was exactly what I remembered. But I think I finally saw him for himself."

Holden let a breath out, relieved.

"Will there be a second date?"

"No," I said smoothly, smiling back at him.

"Okay. Besides, he has been married for the past two years. So that would have made things awkward."

"Why didn't you tell me?!"

Holden shrugged, "I guess I hoped that he would tell you himself."

I shook my head, not surprised that his cheating ways had endured.

"I have to ask. How were you guy's friends? You guys couldn't be more different."

Holden let out an embarrassed breath.

"Honestly, it's hard for me to remember. Our parents had been friends, so we were thrown into the same situations a lot. I was a little shy, and it was easier to hold onto pre-made friendships. But he was an asshole and proved that to me more than once."

"How?"

He blushed but answered my question.

"Well, for one. Over you."

"Me?" I asked, confused.

As far as I could remember, Ken had introduced us.

104

"Back in 9th grade, you were in my English class. I had a huge crush on you. When I told Ken I wanted to ask you out that summer, he did it before I had a chance."

My mouth dropped open and despite myself, my stomach clenched in hurt. Ken had been my first love. I would have never guessed that he asked me out initially as a way to be a jerk to one of his friends.

"He wasn't interested in me?" I asked in a small voice.

Holden heard how it had sounded and leaned forward.

"Of course, he was. He asked you out for that reason, but it was easy for him to fall for you. I think he loved you as much as he would ever be capable of."

I sank in my chair, thinking of how many times he cheated and lied to me.

"Still not very much though. Or very well."

"Some people aren't capable of much, no matter how great the person they love is."

I gave him a small grin. Holden looked like he was trying to build himself up for a moment before giving me a funny look.

"But you know, waiting can have its perks. You dated the jerk and knew what it was like to not be treated well. And now he's alone or with a wife he is lying to, and I'm here with you."

I giggled a little, he was apparently trying very hard to flirt but was so nervous it was a little ridiculous.

"That's true."

He cautiously leaned over and held my hand. I let him, knitting our fingers together.

"Would it be okay if I kissed you?" he asked quietly.

I looked over at him and wondered how long he had wanted to. I had a feeling it went all the way back to that 9th grade English class and was touched by that.

I wasn't sure how much I would be able to give him. The sadness that I carried still felt like an extra pair of skin I wore regularly.

Despite that, I leaned forward. I was drowning in my pain, but when our lips came together under the fireworks, my heart finally understood the excitement of bursting in the sky and the fear of not knowing how to fall.

*

"Hello?"

CJ poked his head into the front door.

"Hey, in here," I called from the kitchen.

I was attempting to outline my next book, but it was impossible. I was supposed to be editing my current manuscript, and the guilt was killing me. I had obligations to Rusty and my editor.

CJ came in and hugged Macy, who was sitting at the counter eating a Greek yogurt.

"What's up?" she asked, offering him a bite.

He took the spoon, scooped up a huge bite, then handed it back to her.

"Nothing. I am at the end of my CD's, so I was going to look through Terry's. I want to keep the music varied. I'm thinking she's searching for a particular beat. You know she could never resist dancing to Joan Jett."

Macy laughed, "Oh yeah. She would dance in the grocery store if anything from the 80's came onto the stereo system."

"Exactly. How are you doing?"

She sighed, "I'm okay. I can't wait until Terry is home and things can get back to some kind of normal."

My hands stilled over my keyboard. I got that this wasn't supposed to be a permanent situation. But, a part of me didn't want Macy to miss Terry if it meant that she wished she was here instead of me.

I missed Terry so much, but I still wanted a place for myself here. When Terry came back would they assume that I wanted to leave? Without Mom to hold us together would they even want me here at all?

Macy spun off of her seat and headed downstairs with CJ. A couple minutes later CJ came back upstairs and sat at the table with me. I took a deep breath and shut the computer, giving up on working for the day.

"What about you? How are you doing?" CJ asked.

I shrugged.

"The same. I'm visiting Ter as much as possible. But it's tough seeing her like that. I'm glad you are going as well. She isn't alone often."

He leaned back in his chair.

"You know I love her. But it's more than that." "What do you mean?"

I could see his throat working, and his eyes seemed overfull.

"That night... She wanted to go home. I convinced her to go out with me, dancing. She was going through a lot the last couple months, and she needed to let her hair down. I encouraged her to let her guard down."

I shook my head, "I don't understand."

"She had been stressed out over a patient."

"Gina?" I asked.

His eyes widened slightly.

"She told you?"

"No, I found some information on my mom's computer. I was super confused. But I think her boyfriend Lucas might be the person who hit us."

"We thought it was over. Gina's brother recently committed suicide, and I believed that he was who she had seen in her vision. I told her it was over. And she stopped looking over her shoulder. And then..."

He put his head in his hands. I leaned forward to console him.

"It's not your fault that Lucas hurt her. My mom once told me that when visions were put into motion, it meant that the person's mind was made up. It's unpredictable how it will all play out until it's too late. But she wouldn't blame you."

He looked down, and I could tell he would never forgive himself. My stomach burned. CJ had known and still wasn't able to help. But he wasn't psychic.

How much would I have been able to do if I had moved home sooner? Would I have gotten my gift earlier? Would I have been able to use it to save my mom's life?

*

Getting through my manuscript was harder than I imagined. When I pictured editing it for publication, I always seemed to be wearing a cardigan, sipping white wine and relaxing to Bob Marley.

Instead, I was sitting in the near dark, dressed in a tattered sweatshirt, and sweating for the nervousness building in my stomach.

My book was about a pair of little boys, childhood friends, or rather was inspired by real ones. One night they are playing on the roof of the clubhouse in the main characters backyard, a club house belonging to Rusty. There is a terrible accident, and Rusty dies.

I know the death scene is coming up and I want more than anything to not experience it.

My last interaction with my manuscript included Rusty himself throwing it at me, demanding I rewrote the ending. He told me I abandoned him. As I got closer to the scene, I knew something was going to happen. Something was close, and it was out of my realm.

I took a deep breath and plowed forward. As I read, the memories filtered through my mind. Rusty jumps from the ledge of the clubhouse, planning a perfect cannonball into his pool below.

For one second, he is weightless before plummeting to the ground. He is motionless and his friend, Len, runs inside to tell his mom. His mom's bedroom door is locked, and she isn't alone. I set my file folder down on my desk and reach for my root beer.

As my hands closed over the can, an ice-cold hand covers mine. I scream as I look up, taking in the bloated face and fish bitten jaw line.

The woman in front of me backs up into the shadows of the corner of my room. I covered my mouth with shaking hands, trying to take a deep breath to hold back my vomit. I could smell the lake water coming off of her, I could still see her soggy sneakers peeking out of the shadow hanging against my back wall.

"I didn't mean to scare you. I thought this was... okay. I'm sorry, I don't know...." she said in a whispery tenor.

"No," I said, taking a step closer and forcing myself to look at her.

She seemed unsure and stayed in the dark.

"Are you here for me?" I asked, not knowing how to start a conversation with a ghost.

I had known Rusty since I was a child. It felt natural. But this was the first time I had communicated with anyone else since receiving my full gift.

"I thought you could help me. I feel like you have helped my son."

"Rusty? Rusty is your son?" I asked, sitting back down in my chair and cradling my soda.

She shimmered with purpose, "I'm Caroline."

Goosebumps broke out on my arms as I heard her name out loud, one I had written down in the book behind me. A character I thought I had created standing in front of me.

She looked so different than Rusty. When I was little Rusty was vibrant, so close to being an angel. Now he looked tired and darker, but this was something new. Caroline didn't need to tell me that she had drowned. She was wearing the evidence of her death; she was wearing her last moments as a shroud.

"I'm trying to help Rusty. I knew him when I was younger and recently moved back home. He is upset with me. See I wrote a book, a book about him. But I didn't know it was about him," I told her, holding my manuscript and wondering if I should extend it to her.

"He is upset?" Caroline asked.

"Yes, I wrote the wrong ending. I made him a promise when we were kids. A promise to... To find you so that he could move on."

Caroline sunk to the ground, the skin on her legs seemed to emit murky water as she crossed them. I had to swallow hard as I watched the shriveled skin stretch and almost break over her knees.

"I can't see him..."

"Of course, you can. It's all he wanted. He has been waiting here for years."

Suddenly she was standing in front of me, tipping my chair back and screaming into my face.

"Don't you think I would go to him if I could? I am not saying I don't want to, you dumb bitch. I am saying I can't. I can't see him. I am like this because I made a mistake. Because he died."

Trembling I tipped my chair back up, and Caroline slipped back into the corner.

"I don't understand," I said quietly.

I wished more than ever my mom was here to explain how all of this worked.

"He is dead because of me. I don't get closure. I get pain."

With a sound that could only be explained as all of the air being sucked out of the room, I was alone again. Slowly the sound came back in a whining tone, then exploded.

All of the photos smashed off my wall, the glass flying inches from my face. The books shot off the shelves, and the shelves themselves lost their backs.

I screamed, running out of the room.

*

"Claire, this is insane," Ash told me.

She was sweeping up the glass on my bedroom floor and shaking her head.

"No shit. I thought you were all excited by this. You thought That this was going to be fun and that we would get a new TV show where you were my sidekick."

Ash rolled her eyes at me.

"Okay. Maybe I didn't think about this part of it. The scary ones."

"You have no idea." Ash sat on the bed, tying the trash bag full of glass and broken frames.

"Well, she was obviously an angry spirit."

"Well, yes, Ash. She was angry."

"That's not what I mean. Have you done any research since getting your gift? The internet is full of fantastic information."

I sat down, gesturing for her to go on.

"Angry spirits are people who died traumatically. Their souls are fractured, so they get stuck in their death state and have a hard time moving on. I bet you anything Caroline literally can't see Rusty because it would help her move on and this is her punishment."

"What could she have done?" I asked, glancing towards my manuscript.

Ash followed my gaze, "Your guess is better than mine."

I sat on my hands, refusing to touch the stack of paper again.

"I am scared to try to read it. Every time I pick it up something crazy happens. It's terrifying."

She sighed, "It looks like that's your only choice though. Rusty made you read it for a reason. There's something you don't know."

Part of me wondered if I was avoiding reading because it took my focus away from what was going on with Terry. This wasn't the only unanswered question hanging over our life, more like one of a million.

Another part of me wondered if it was guilt keeping me from my book. I was disgusted with the idea of writing over Rusty's life, making an ending that wasn't as painful. It was completely disrespectful to what he had gone through.

I had neglected him, Terry, Macy, and my mom. I was unable to save anyone.

*

Grocery shopping was so much easier now that Macy and I had truly broken the ice with one another. When I first moved in, cooking was so depressing. I did not know where anything was. I hated that I was so unfamiliar with the place where my mom and sisters had spent so much time.

After my talk with Macy, I had woken up in the middle of the night and gone through the kitchen completely. I looked through every cupboard, every drawer. I never wanted to go to the wrong place while looking for spatulas again.

But I what I found was so much better. I found my mother's junk drawer.

She was such a clean person but ended up having these little pockets of odds and ends. Pens, random receipts, candles, batteries, even some Halloween gift bags that looked like they were from our elementary school days. I found cookbooks in the pantry with my mom's notes written in the margins.

I brought every single one back to my bedroom and read through them. Recipes adjusted to what she found worked, ingredients added and omitted, and a review of the ones she had tried. The personal notes were my favorite.

Perfect for when Terry has a cold. She ate three bowls of this soup when she had strep throat!

Macy and I adored these coconut cupcakes! Do not throw away the extra frosting. It's also delicious spread on muffins. Or just on a spoon when you feel like breaking your diet in the middle of the night.

Pair this cornbread with the chili mom showed you how to make. Claire really enjoyed this. Next time, drizzle honey on top and send some home with her!

I wanted to cook these recipes. To remember what she remembered. To add my own notes. I touched the grooves where her pen had etched in her words and felt close to her for the first time in years. I would be able to carry on a piece of her memory.

In this way, shopping was finally bearable. As I was comparing whole wheat and traditional macaroni noodles, someone bumped into my cart. I turned, annoyed until I saw that it was Holden.

"Hey!" he said with a huge grin.

"Hey, are you just clocking in?"

"Out, actually. Do you need any help?"

"Nope. I'm almost done."

He grinned, untying his apron.

112

"Are you interested in taking a walk after this? It's a beautiful day outside, and I have had way too much fluorescent light today."

I laughed, "Sure. Let me finish up, and I will meet you outside in ten minutes."

After I checked out Holden helped me put the groceries in the trunk. Then, he took my hand and led me to a small but lush park across the street. It was hot, but the breeze was somehow cooler underneath the shade of the huge oak trees.

"Do you do this often?" I asked.

"Not usually after work in the afternoon. But I love to take walks after working the night shift. The air by the pond smells really sweet, and it feels fresh here even in the middle of August."

I could imagine, I remembered how unbearable summer could be. The year they repaved most of the streets in the town center I had avoided the mall for months. The sun reflected off the new black top, baking everyone and making everything sticky.

"Did you ever want to leave Spokane? To go to college and try living somewhere else?" I asked.

Holden thought for a moment. I appreciated that he took my questions seriously, even if they were about something simple.

"When I was in high school it was definitely on my mind a lot. But the summer we graduated my dad got cancer."

"I'm so sorry. I had no idea."

He gave me a sad smile.

"He got better. Even so, he needed help at the store. He never asked, but my path was chosen. I guess I could have fought it and been upset. But he's my dad. The more time I put into his store, the more I felt like this is where I was meant to be. I grew to love it."

His selflessness amazed me and also made me a little ashamed of how much I had avoided being a part of my family.

Yet, just being here made me feel like it was never too late. Being here for Macy was where I was meant to be. It was hard but right.

"What about you? Do you miss school?"

I shook my head.

"I had fun, but I was ready for it to end. I always meant to move back. I want to travel someday, but this was always where I wanted to raise my family. I loved growing up here."

"Me too."

We walked until we reached the pond then sat on a bench together.

"What do you plan on doing for work? Your degree is in Creative Writing? Will you teach?"

"That was the plan... but then," I paused.

I had been keeping my news close to my chest, but Holden made it easy to want to tell him the whole truth.

"I wrote a book while in college and just found out that it was accepted for publication."

His eyes widened, and he squeezed my hand.

"That's incredible."

"Thank you."

He leaned back, "That seems to fit you so well. I remember you reading all the time in school. While walking to classes, during football games, I remember you even mentioning you brought a book to a house party."

I laughed.

"Well yeah. One can only dance for so long. What if I got bored?"

Holden looked at his watch.

"I need to say goodbye so I can run some errands for my mom. But I am going to ask you on a date. Will you say yes?"

I beamed, loving that he was asking for permission to ask.

"I think you have some pretty good odds."

*

I had been waiting for Rusty for the past three days, and he wasn't coming. I felt frustrated, unable to send out my psychic vibes to let him know that I was ready to talk. Taking one last stab at communication, I went to where I knew he hung out the most when we were kids.

Crossing my legs, I settled in front of the club house. He had always enjoyed interrupting me while I read and begging me to read it out loud. It looked like times hadn't changed at all. Rusty appeared at my side, tipping my book so that he could see the words on the page.

"I always wondered, can you read?" I asked, handing him the book.

"I was learning. I can write my name," he said, glowing like his old self for a second before turning wispy and dark again.

I smiled at him.

"This is the Tale of Two Cities. Do you remember it? I had to read it for school and read every chapter aloud to you."

He leaned his head against my arm, smiling back.

"Did you read the ending of your book?" he asked, flipping through the novel we once experienced together.

"Yes, the ending wasn't what I remembered. The very last chapter was of you coming back and getting to see your parents one last time. Them being able to see you as an angel brings them back together, and they fall back in love."

My hands were sweaty as I watch him process the ending, I had written for him. I was surprised when he seemed to blush.

"I wanted to tell you I was sorry. For yelling at you."

"It's okay Rusty."

"No, I think this is my fault. That's the ending I wanted more than anything. I wanted to find her so that I could tell her that I was sorry and that it wasn't her fault. Do you think that they broke up?" he asked, tears welling in his eyes.

My throat started to close a tiny bit as I understood that he has been searching for her as a living soul all this time. I couldn't make myself answer him yet.

Something else had started to sink in. Rusty wasn't stuck in his death state, but Caroline was.

"Rusty, how did you die? In my book, I write that it's from falling off the club house. Do you remember?"

He closed his eyes, breathing deeply.

"Can I take you somewhere?" he whispered.

I took his little hand, almost being able to feel his skin in the palm of my hand. I followed him three blocks down from our house to the pond. The deck had been renovated before we moved to this part of town and the wood shone from last night's drizzle.

The pond wasn't huge but was still a favorite for fishing and was stocked twice a year. Since it was a weekday, the pond was empty at the moment. As we reached the dock, Rusty veered off to the side and sat on the grass.

"Did you come here when you were alive?" I asked.

Rusty smiled, letting himself remember.

"All the time. Aside from the club house, it was my special place. My daddy and I fished every morning for the whole summer. It was my favorite."

My eyes got watery again. I could see him so clearly it broke my heart.

"I remember being here that night."

"At the pond?" I asked, confused.

My vision showed him dying from the fall. But his mom had obviously drowned to death. I wondered if he was seeing her death. If he was being brought here over and over as a way to be close to her.

"Claire... is my mom gone?" he asked, his voice breaking.

I wanted to believe that he was asking me if she moved away. But we both knew that he hadn't been able to feel her here or anywhere else for a long time.

And now I knew it was because she wasn't allowed. I wondered if I was ever going to be able to close that door for him.

"Yes," I told him quietly, forcing myself not to look away.

He shuddered violently, already expecting my answer. He cried freely, sobs shaking his thin little body. I opened my arms, and he curled up in my lap.

I cried with him, for everything he lost and what could never be.

"But your daddy, Rusty. Your daddy is still here," I said, rubbing his back.

"Help me find him, Claire."

"Of course. I promise."

He sighed, seeming relieved.

"I feel like I am fading away. The shadows make me so tired."

My arms broke out in goosebumps.

"The shadows?"

"The shadows that move in the house. It's hard to rest when they are there. They are growing. Guard your heart. They are scary."

If Rusty had seen shadows as well, it wasn't my imagination. There was something dark in the house. But what?

He leaned into my arms, shivering. I don't know how long we sat there together. I'm not sure if he had resolved to try to find her in the world that he lived in, but his hand was even more solid than before.

*

"What about chemistry?" he asked, flipping through the class catalog.

"I took chemistry last year," Macy replied, not looking up.

My stomach flip flopped as their awkwardness with each other filled up the room. I wanted to blame my mom for that, for how far my dad had drifted away. I wondered why Macy had never reached out.

But then I thought back to my years in college, how many letters my mom had sent me and gift packages that I had opened ungraciously. Complaining about the fact that she didn't know what kind of shampoo I used or that I wasn't eating carbs to avoid gaining the freshmen fifteen.

But standing here, draining noodles and adding the sauce, I realized that she had never stopped reaching out. I had stopped responding. The only parent I spent time with was the one that gave me the least of themselves. It didn't make any sense.

My throat tightened as my eyes threatened to flood over.

"Did we remember parmesan?" Macy asked me from the table.

I took a deep breath and collected myself.

"Yep."

I made three plates and set them on the table as Macy gathered up her books to make room. We powered through a quiet dinner and at the end I watched Macy stiffly kiss Dad on the cheek.

Back in the car I couldn't help but ask, "Mac. Do you hate him?"

She turned to me, stunned.

"Of course not. I love Dad. Why would you ask me that?"

I shrugged.

"You guys are so weird together."

She sighed.

"I honestly hardly notice it anymore. Dad isn't a super involved parent."

I blushed, feeling responsible for some reason.

"Does that upset you?"

She shook her head.

"No. I think he does the best that he can. I believe that he loved being a husband and when that didn't work out, he was afraid to let anyone else in. I think that he loves us as much as he can. I don't expect anything more from him, and I don't feel like he expects anything from me."

I couldn't help remembering that Holden had said something similar about Ken. That some people are only able to love you as much as they are capable of. How sometimes their level of love isn't up to your standard.

Macy seemed to know that Holden had popped into my head because she gave me a funny smile. I blushed involuntarily.

"I think he would have been able to open himself up more if he had fallen in love again. I remember being at one of his work parties and there were at least three divorcees there that he had a compatible aura with."

I chuckled, thinking of what my dad would have thought if Macy had tried to set up our father based on auras.

"Can you see your own? Yours and Britney's together?" I asked.

"No. I wish. I have to rely on the chemistry that you can pick up on otherwise. And I love her."

I looked at her and was envious of how easily she could say that. I knew she meant it and was so happy for her.

"But you know whose aura I can see as plain as day? Yours. It's a beautiful teal green and very strong."

"What does that mean?" I asked, laughing a little bit.

"It can mean a lot of things. But the most interesting part is that I have never seen a shade of green quite like yours. Until I met Holden."

I snorted, and Macy grinned at me triumphantly. She obviously had been keeping that information for an opportune moment and was enjoying watching me squirm.

"And?" I said, turning away and focusing on the road.

"And, I think that you're an idiot for ignoring the natural chemistry."

I shrugged but couldn't get what she said out of my head. I felt the chemistry. But maybe I was a little bit like Dad. It was hard to love someone when the world was telling me so loudly that love can bring so much heartbreak.

*

When I was growing up, I woke up in the middle of the night often. But sometimes only my mind would be aware that I was awake.

I would lay there with my eyes open and feel an immense pressure on my chest. My arms and legs would remain completely immobile like I was unconscious but instead I was trapped. I would force myself to take deep breaths and eventually my arms and legs would tingle before beginning to move again.

It was something that had happened so much as I was growing up but stopped as soon as I moved out. But here I was, five years later, trapped inside of my body once again.

As I laid there frozen, I looked around my room. Everything was exactly the same as it had been back then. At 14 I felt the pressure and chalked it up to panic. Now I knew it was because those that couldn't be seen were tired of being invisible.

A shadow darkened my doorway. The door was cracked, and it slowly swung open. The shadow crossed the threshold, and with a

119

pounding heart, I watched it make its way over to my bed. I wanted to thrash, to scream, but I was locked inside of myself.

The dark form stood at the side of my bed, wispy pieces of black stealing over the sheet and stopping just short of my arm. I could feel the cold, the pain. It wasn't dark because it was angry. It was dark because it was void of anything. There was no light in these spirits. These spirits needed to fill something up to be whole.

The shadow moved like a spider down to my blanket, and slowly it began pulling it towards my head. I could feel the blanket catch on my night shirt and then get jerked upwards. My body that was covered by the blanket pressed into the bed, and I knew it wasn't just a blanket covering it.

Something was under the blanket with me, only able to hold me down while hidden in the shadows. The blanket was inches from my face, and I could hear a slight hissing coming from underneath.

My arms and legs began to feel like they held static and I twitched my hand. All at once I was able to move again and threw the blanket off of me. An uninterrupted darkness enveloped my body before evaporating violently.

I gasped, leaped off of my bed, and ran into the hall.

Macy's door was open, and I jogged through it. I quietly closed the door and jumped into bed with her. She roused slightly, glanced at me, and then rolled over. I faced the door, waiting to see if the darkness returned.

The only thing that was angry in this house seemed to be Caroline. How fractured was her spirit? Was this what she became when the sun went down?

*

"I am close to being done editing it, and then I will be sending it back to my publisher. In any other situation, this would be a time to start planning a party... But that just feels wrong. Maybe I will bring some champagne back here, and you and I can give Macy her first glass," I told Terry, massaging her hand and straightening her thin blanket.

"Oh, you know that Macy has already had her first glass. She's probably had more than we really want to know about."

I jumped and spun around. Terry, wispy and slightly blue, sat on the couch that was next to the window overlooking the parking lot.

"Ter," I said.

I swung my head back and forth, looking at Terry lying in bed and somehow also sitting on the couch.

"It's okay."

"Where are you? Does this mean you are dying?" I asked, my throat growing tighter.

Terry looked around her, "I kind of just feel here... I am not going anywhere, but I am not really part of this room either."

I had wanted to talk to her, to touch her, but now that she was here, I was stunned silent.

"You really did get a beautiful gift, Claire. Why did you hide it for so long?" she asked.

I began to cry quietly.

"Because Dad needed me to. But it was a mistake. And now it's too late."

"No, it's not. You are still on the path that was always meant for you."

"Ter, what am I supposed to be doing? Is Lucas going to hurt us? How do I make sure that Macy will be safe?"

Terry leaned forward.

"I can't really talk about that or even see it. I am not in heaven; I am right here. Waiting for whatever comes next. But I had to tell you. There is a cost to these gifts."

"Costs?"

"Beautiful gifts have a very high price tag."

She started to swirl and slowly fade away, leaving only a faint steam behind. I laid my head on my arms and cried.

If this wasn't the cost, seeing the hole my mom left and my sister comatose, I didn't think I could take whatever came next.

Chapter Ten

Claire

"Hey," Ash said, coming into the living room and plopping down on the couch next to me.

"Hi," I responded, shutting my computer and setting it next to me.

"I thought you were going to the cemetery today?" she asked.

I sighed.

"I did. But it was awful, so I came home."

"Was it too hot outside? I almost wanted to wear a tank top today."

"No, not the weather. Just how empty it feels there. I keep trying to open myself up so that I can feel my mom in any way. I don't feel her there. I don't feel her at the nursing home. I don't feel her at home. All that's there is her too shiny gravestone next to an empty plot. It seems like a spot waiting for Terry."

Her eyes clouded and she covered my hand with hers. I gave her a small smile then gestured towards the manuscript I could see sticking out of her purse.

"Did you read it?" I asked.

She took it out and laid it on the coffee table.

"I did."

"And? What am I missing?"

Ash leaned back and gave me a grin.

"You are truly the worst psychic in the world. It's super clear that when you are reading, you see it through author's eyes. You are not letting yourself see the whole story."

I raised my eyebrow at her, more hurt than I wanted to be.

"Worst psychic? I'm new."

She waved my excuses away, "You're avoiding the whole story."

"Then what's the story, Ash?"

"Let's start with the questions. Have you done any research at all?"

I shook my head, knowing she was right. I was avoiding everything about this half ass's investigation even though my heart completely broke for Rusty.

"What questions?"

"Okay. Caroline blames herself for Rusty's death. Why? Where was she when Rusty was playing outside? When he falls, his friend runs inside and finds her door locked. You imply that she wasn't alone and that she was hiding something from her family. Was it the guilt over whatever her secret was that made her lose it altogether?"

"In real life you mean? I don't know. When I was writing, I didn't try to delve that far into the parent's backstory. I wanted her and the husband to have a happy ending."

"Okay, I accept that. But what about how quickly she decides he is dead? She sees him lying on the ground, and that sight alone sends her off the deep end?"

I stared at her, "Are you implying I didn't murder him... Enough?"

"No, the whole situation is so terrible already. But that's not the real story. We know they lived here when Rusty died. Let's Google for deaths in town over the past twenty years. Something like a little kid dying and the mom drowning would make the local news for sure. It had to be more than him falling from the clubhouse roof. It had to have been something that traumatized her to the point where she had a nervous breakdown."

I pulled my laptop back onto my lap. After trying out a couple different phrases, a news story popped up from before we moved to our house. A local woman drives off a dock at the pond with her son in the car.

"This has to be it," Ash says, turning the computer to read the whole article.

"Caroline was obviously having an affair. When she wasn't paying attention, Rusty died, and she blamed herself. She couldn't handle it. So, she killed herself went to her grave with Rusty by her side," I said, disgusted with the visions filling my head.

123

"Your right, I was having an affair," says a voice from the corner of the room.

I scream involuntarily, making Ash drop my laptop.

"What the hell, Claire."

I see Caroline's wet sneaker peeking from behind the living room curtains, her puffy fingers wrapping over the edge of the purple satin that my mom picked out four years ago.

I squeezed Ash's hand, "Can you see her?"

Ash followed my gaze to the curtains, "She's here? Caroline?" I nodded slowly.

I watched goose bumps break out over Ash's arm, and she leaned slightly back. The last time I talked to Caroline, she destroyed my room. I hoped she wasn't going to throw a tantrum in here because Terry spent a good $1500 on the TV propped up next to the bookshelves.

"It was too much. It was my fault. I could have left my husband and been with the person I thought I loved. Instead, I lost the person I loved more than anything in the world."

"You did it while Rusty was playing outside?" I asked, trying not to sound accusatory.

"It was the perfect arrangement. He was Len's father."

Hearing Len's name out loud in Caroline's voice sent a snapping noise through the air, and even Ash flinched from the change in the room's atmosphere.

"Is she gone?" Ash asked me.

The whining sound was back, so I leaned forward and put my head in my hands. Len. Len. Len. I knew that name more than just as a character that was connected to Rusty.

I let out a little whimper as vivid memories pushed themselves into my head. A teenager that used to talk to me when I was playing at the pond. He was beautiful with sandy blonde hair and the creamiest skin I had ever seen.

When I was 11, I had such a crush on him. I spent time with him until I was 15. He was the first person that I ever loved in that way, and I thought he loved me back. I had my first kiss with him. It never occurred to me to wonder why he never got older.

124

When my parents divorced, I came to the understanding that loving the boy who lived at the lake might cost me my dad's love. So, I stopped going. When I was 16, I revisited the lake and he was gone. I mourned him privately and was so ashamed.

"Len," I say out loud.

"Rusty's friend?"

I sat up, taking a deep breath.

"Caroline was having an affair with Len's dad. They would sleep together while the boys played outside."

Her jaw dropped open slightly, and she looked carefully at me.

"But that's not all, is it?" she asked.

I looked at her, embarrassed for some reason. Which was ridiculous when I considered that she had just watched me talk to a ghost in my living room. I was suddenly struck by the overwhelming realization that this was what I was most afraid of.

Someone finding out that I was different and hating me because that's what happened to my mom. Ash not only knew, but she also accepted me entirely.

"I used to see Len too. When I was 11, I met him at the pond. I guess I loved him. He was who I had my first kiss with."

She raised her eyebrows, smiling a little.

"I remember that. I thought he was someone who only lived here for a summer. You never talked about him again."

"My parents divorced that summer, so I stopped going to see him. I didn't want my dad to know. I guess I stopped seeing everyone and everything that summer."

Ash gave me a sad nod.

"You believe me? That I knew him in another way?"

"Of course."

I leaned forward, pulling her into a hug. She hugged back, laying her head on my shoulder.

"We will figure this out, Claire."

I took a deep breath, allowing myself to believe this was true for the first time in a long time. I wasn't alone.

*

If you didn't count the catastrophe with Ken, I hadn't been on a date in almost a year. My senior year of college had been occupied fully by finishing my book, and I didn't worry about it.

But now a year felt like such a long time because, tonight was the night I went out with Holden for the first time.

We spent many nights together with friends in school, but this was different. This time I knew how he felt about me and the responsibility of his high expectations made me so nervous. How I felt made me nervous.

I wanted him to fall for me because every day that we spent time together, I could feel myself spiraling into teenage lust. It was scary, wanting him this early into getting to know him.

Holden was teaching me that I was completely wrong about love. Love wasn't about how long you have known a person; love was about connecting in a way that you couldn't put into words. If I felt this way about him now, how would I handle anything deeper?

For my entire life, I have shied away from honest relationships. But I had a feeling that would be impossible with Holden. He wouldn't let me hide my true self from him.

"Macy!" I called, sticking my head out of my bedroom door.

I watched her bounce her way out of her room, her pink cell phone plastered to her ear.

"Will you help me pick out an outfit? I'm going to dinner with Holden tonight."

She gave me an excited look.

"I will call you later, Brit. Claire has a fashion emergency... Love you too."

I laughed, "I wouldn't call it an emergency."

"I would," she said, setting her phone on my desk and walking over to my closet.

"Where are you going?" she asked.

"I think we are checking out the Bite of Spokane, with all of the food trucks."

"Very cool." S

he quickly pulled out my favorite skinny jeans, a vintage Beatles T-shirt that she bought for me last fall, a black pearl necklace, and shiny black flats. I had stared into my closet for an hour and didn't see this outfit put together. She was the best.

As I got dressed, she went back to my desk and started flipping through my photo albums. Then, she picked up my manuscript. I hadn't been brave enough to tell her about my gift, but my publisher calling so often made it impossible not to tell her about my book.

She was sad that I didn't tell her but when I explained that I got the news the same night of the accident she was surprisingly gracious.

"Is this it?" she asked.

I gripped the shirt, nervous to see it in her hands. But the air didn't change, and the others in the house seemed quiet for the moment.

"Can I read it? I haven't read any of your work since that cancer story you wrote in elementary school."

I laughed, remembering the pretentious but beloved first novel I ever wrote. I suddenly also remembered Macy writing a pretend review for it and sliding it under my bedroom door. I had it taped into a scrapbook somewhere.

An hour later I was at Riverton Park with Holden, holding his hand casually as we perused the food stalls. When we paid our way in, we were given five tickets. Each ticket got you a small dish at each stall, and then you voted on your favorite before leaving. It was such a fun way to try out different local places without having to buy a whole meal.

At least half were cupcake trucks, and I really wanted to try a burger before the night was through.

"Have you tried Cake Kiss?" I asked Holden.

I handed the girl at the booth my ticket and grabbed a piece of Salted Caramel cake.

"No, but that looks great."

He gave her a ticket as well and took a slice of Amaretto cheesecake.

"Okay. But now that you grabbed a different flavor, the rules are that you have to share at least one bite so that we can experience as many different types of food as possible."

He laughed, "That's the official rules?"

"Well yeah. Didn't you see the sign when we walked in?"

He gave me an incredulous look but offered his fork to me.

I rolled my eyes, "I'm not four. I can steal a bite all on my own."

I leaned into him and took a huge forkful of his cheesecake. He scoffed and took an even bigger piece of mine. As we walked around, I told him about editing my book, my last year of school, Macy's upcoming orientation for pep squad.

He made me laugh with a million stories about working in the grocery store. We had a group of pranksters in town that had been arranging different signs to spell out dirty words and elderly women kept seeming to find them before Holden did. They were horrified but then kept asking him to explain what some of the words meant.

As we sat down with what we thought were the tastiest burgers at the festival, I realized that I hadn't been sad all day long. A part of me felt horribly guilty for being out on a date, living my life when I was supposed to be searching for those who had lost that privilege.

"Do you ever think about high school?" Holden asked me, mixing salt and pepper into his ketchup.

I laughed, "More these days than I really want to. Since Macy found out you went to school with me, she dragged out all my old photo albums and yearbooks. I have had way too many emo jokes this last week. Enough to last a lifetime."

"Were you really that emo?" he said, laughing.

"My eyeliner definitely suggested so. Why do you ask? Is it on your mind a lot?"

He sat back, chewing a huge bite of his bacon and pineapple burger on a pretzel bun.

"I just wonder a lot. If we knew what we knew now, would our lives have turned out any different? Would you have looked at me differently?" he asked, blushing a little.

128

I smiled, trying to imagine what that would have been like. Knowing that the guy I spent my high school dances with and kissed after school had really cared about me. Not spending every single night worrying about what people thought of me. Or, crying as much because Holden would have never cheated on me.

Would we have stayed together throughout college? Would he have made sure I spent more time with my mom and sisters? Would we have been getting married this summer?

I wondered if my mom would have had a chance to spend time with him if she would have seen a future for us. She had hated Ken. In fact, once she saw that he was going to dump me in a vision and had been a little bit too happy.

She kept implying that I should take the hint. That if someone kept leaving you then maybe you needed to move on. Back then I had always used it as another reason to believe that she didn't know me at all. But maybe she had seen something I hadn't.

Maybe she had seen that I was wasting my time because my real future was already so close.

"I see you now," I said quietly.

He looked up, smiling, before gently kissing me on the cheek. This was so much easier than my relationship with Ken was. My mom always told me that it was supposed to be that way.

She would have liked him so much. My stomach fluttered as I was struck with the certain knowledge that that yes, our lives would have gone in an entirely different direction. We would have ended up together and never looked back.

This felt like a second chance and a part of me wanted to pull back from that. I didn't know if I deserved to start feeling better when my mom wouldn't be able to watch me turn into who she hoped I would be.

*

As I relearned this house, I found so many past fears. There were certain parts of the house where I had always been afraid. I didn't see anything in the darkness then, but that was when I was still sheltered by my veil.

Now those past fears that my dad called silly were all I thought about when I was home alone. There weren't just dark corners to walk past quickly. I caught sudden flashes of white hands reaching around corners, shadows as someone waited outside of every single door I closed. I heard people clear their throat while I loaded the dishwasher and was afraid to turn around.

Macy was spending the night with a couple of friends from pep squad, so I had the house to myself this weekend. I felt like I was 11 again and was very close to asking Ash to come stay with me.

Last night I was reading, and a huge rush of hot breath blew against my ear. It was so loud that I had to stifle a scream. I had looked all over the room, but no one was there. I had slept with the light on.

Washing laundry was the worst. I had hated this room growing up. A big window was the only source of light, so shadows had always darkened at least half of the room after 1 pm. I was taking deep breaths and trying to think of anything but the last James Wan movie as I finished up the last load of towels.

As I shut the clear dryer door, legs reflected back at me. The hair on the back of my neck stood on end as I stared at them. The legs were muscular and wearing gray slacks. I glanced down at my own legs clad in yoga pants.

I slowly looked back up to see that the legs were closer than a second ago. Before I could get the guts up to turn fingers brushed my upper arms. I could feel breathing on the back of my shoulders.

"Where am I?" a voice asked, sounding like they were speaking through gauze.

My voice stuck in my throat as the hands tightened. Then they were gone, and the room's temperature grew warmer. I forced myself to walk back to my room at a normal pace then grabbed my cell phone.

"Hey, Ash. How do you feel about sleeping over?"

*

"Are we supposed to plant flowers in the summer? I feel like Mom always did this in the early spring."

I shrugged.

"So, they wilt early. That's okay. Our backyard will be beautiful for about a month, and then all the leaves will fall. Then it will be beautiful in a different way."

Macy looked up, then over my shoulder.

"Do we have a new neighbor?"

I turned around and saw a small woman standing by our fence, her hands gripping it and her eyes darting around nervously.

"Hi," I said, standing up and walking over to her.

"Hi, is this the house of... Is this where Terry lives?"

I straightened. My chest tightened as I recognized her from Terry's files. Gina's face was partially shown in one of the hospital photos.

"Yes. Can I help you?" I said, trying not to scare her off.

"Um, I'm not sure. My name's Gina. I called about a week ago."

Macy joined us.

"Yeah. That was me. I'm Macy, this is Claire. We're Terry's sisters."

Gina looked at the house behind us.

"Is she home yet?"

I shook my head, "No, she is still in a coma."

Gina's eyes darted crazily, and her hands shook.

"Why don't you come inside? I'll make you a cup of coffee? Or tea?" I asked, taking her hand gently and opening up the gate.

Once inside Gina seemed to collapse into an armchair. She looked like she was going to pass out at any moment.

"I'm not trying to put you on the spot, but why are you looking for Terry? I was under the impression that she didn't see you as a client anymore," I said.

I handed her a cup of green tea with the bag still seeping.

"I wasn't. But I feel like... No, I know that this is all my fault. And your mom...."

Gina broke off as she burst into tears. Macy's face turned red, and I squeezed her hand. It was hard seeing a complete stranger cry for your family, even if they did feel responsible. I sat down across from her.

"I was there that night. I was in the car."

Gina's eyes widened in terror.

"I saw him... Someone in a truck. The truck slammed on their gas to hit us at full speed. Then he stopped, got out of the car to make sure we were hurt, and then drove off. It was on purpose."

Her sobs grew, and Macy was now crying. I had told the police about the man watching us the night of the accident, but Macy seemed to be fully letting the information sink in for the first time.

"I'm so sorry," Gina said.

"Do you know who did it? The police ruled it as a hit and run."

Gina blinked frantically.

"It was him. It was Lucas. He tried to kill Terry because she was helping me. My brother committed suicide, and he isn't going to stop until he kills my mom and me. He doesn't care about the money anymore. He wants us dead."

My hands went icy, and the sensation spread throughout my body. It took a while to calm Gina down; it was clear that she was trying to warn us so that we could be on guard. But having her here and feeling like she could have made a difference didn't help at all.

She ended up gathering up her purse, putting her untouched tea on the coffee table and leaving before we could get her phone number or address. Macy was still crying and wrapped her arms around my trembling shoulders.

"She was kind of crazy. And I kind of hate her," Macy said in a bloated voice.

"For what?" I asked, even though I knew the answer.

"For knowing something was wrong and not trying to help. But I am not going to walk away from this. I am going to find Lucas. And I am going to make sure he pays for what he did to our family."

I stood up to embrace her fully.

"You are not doing anything. We are going to find him together. This will end with us. We are going to make sure Mom has justice."

132

*

"No, take it. Macy is at Britney's all day, and there's no way I can eat all of this crap before it gets stale," I told CJ as he raided our pantry.

He grabbed a grocery bag from the shelf where my mom kept them stuffed into a tote and began filling it up with Cheezits and chips. I was only 5'3, and any weight I gained from junk food seemed to settle on my butt. The less we had in the house to tempt me, the better.

"Hey? It's Holden," I heard from the living room.

"In the kitchen," I called, peeking my head out of the pantry.

Holden came around the corner, smiling. How good looking he was still caught me off guard a little bit, and I grinned at him goofily before catching myself.

"Hey, what's up?" I asked.

He held up a paper bag filled with burgers.

"I assumed you hadn't eaten yet and decided to bring you lunch."

"Aw, thank you. You're right. I was cleaning out the pantry today and completely lost track of time."

CJ came out of the pantry with two full bags and tipped his head at Holden. Holden looked at me then back at him, blushing.

"Hey, I'm CJ."

"Hi, I would have bought more if I knew there would be a plus one," Holden said, trying to sound like his happy go lucky self.

I chuckled, and CJ raised his eyebrow at me.

"Nope. That's okay. I only came to get my snack fix. I'm headed to work," CJ leaned over and pecked me on the cheek before letting himself out.

Holden sat at the island, trying to be super casual. I decided to let him simmer. I had never experienced a jealous guy before, and it was more fun than I was willing to admit.

Ken cheated on me so much that I was constantly trailing after him, trying to be what he needed. He didn't need to be jealous of me, I had been his so completely that it was kind of pathetic.

This is how it was supposed to be. I didn't want Holden to be upset, but I did like how desirable I felt at that moment. That I was worth being jealous over.

"A friend of yours?" Holden asked, removing the paper from his burger and staring at it instead of me.

"Something like that," I responded, eating a fry.

"A friend that kisses you. On the cheek."

I shrugged, "I kiss Ash on the cheek."

Holden looked at me, his face still red.

"Well yeah, but Ash doesn't look like that. Ash is a girl."

I laughed, "Calm down, Holden. CJ is Terry's best friend. I have known him since I was in preschool. He's like my big brother and comes from a very snuggly Italian family. He kisses everyone. If he gets to know you, he will probably try kissing your cheek goodbye as well."

He visibly relaxed, and I giggled. Holden shook his head.

"Thank God. It took me years to ask you out. I didn't think I could compete with a guy that looks like that."

I laughed and kissed him on the cheek. He shook his head and pulled me closer.

"No way. Friends kiss on the cheek. I need something better."

*

"And it was able to pull your blanket?" Ash said, hugging a couch pillow to her chest.

I rubbed my arms.

"It wasn't just pulling the blanket. I could hear it kind of whispering to me from underneath. I could feel it pressing down on me."

She shivered, "A shadow?"

I giggled as she pulled out her laptop. Google was her solution to everything. She was known to IMDB a movie before we were even

134

finished watching it, ruining it for the both of us. I sat closer to her to read over her shoulder.

"Shadow figures are supposed to be shades of the underworld. This says that they can shape shift because they aren't human spirits. They are conscious unidimensional beings and perhaps are even demonic."

Ash sat back, and I stared at the screen. It showed a wispy figure caught in the photo, trying to escape out of frame. It was exactly what I saw the other night.

"Demonic?"

"You seem surprised?"

"I kind of thought it was Caroline. Like the fractured part of her, that was angry because she was cut off from Rusty."

"I can see that. But this seems to suggest that they were never human. It says that they usually don't let people see them face to face. If they are sticking around long enough for you to see them, then they are interested in you. That's scary."

"But what am I supposed to do? It's not like I can turn it off."

"Right, but maybe there's a way of building your veil back up and using it like a shield. This is dangerous."

I agreed, but she raised her eyebrows.

"You don't want to?"

"It's just that, I can't close this door right now. What about Rusty? What about helping him? I have ignored him long enough."

She sighed.

"It's a problem, Claire. This isn't hauntings like in the movies. How much are you letting in by being this open?"

Ash was absolutely right. It was terrifying. However, it wasn't only Rusty. I wanted to help him, I needed to help him.

But, I couldn't set up boundaries yet because I might lose a chance to communicate with my mom. I wasn't done with this yet. It was worth it.

*

For our second date, Holden chose a more traditional route, dinner and a movie. We were not planning on going to see an amateur film festival but, didn't realize that it was amateur night until we arrived at the theater.

We chose what we thought was a scary movie. Not only was is not scary, everyone else in the audience was incredibly pretentious and even seemed to be taking notes.

A whole group of hipsters in front of us kept nodding vigorously whenever the main characters used the word lethargic. It was bizarre. At one-point Holden started dozing off. When his head fully hit his chest, I giggled involuntarily. A bunch of people turned around to glare at me.

"I'm sorry," I whispered, trying really hard to repress my smile and not laugh again.

A girl with three eyebrow piercings smirked at me, "We are working to immerse ourselves at this moment. If you can't appreciate what's happening, feel free to leave."

"Thank God," Holden said, standing up loudly and extending his hand to me.

We had powered through three hours of that horrific saga, and now it was way past dinnertime. Most of the traditional restaurants were closed, so we ended up at the Denny's at the end of the street.

"That was awful. I am so sorry," Holden said, holding my hand up and kissing the back of it.

I shrugged, "I've seen worse."

"No. Impossible." "Yes. I hate searching for movies, so I am terrible about not reading the back of cases. I have sat through way too many B horror movies."

Holden laughed, "I certainly don't watch them on purpose. But I have terrible boy taste in movies. Action, corny dialogue, big Michael Bay special effects."

As the waiter came over, Holden shut his menu and put it aside.

"I'm in a dessert before dinner mood. Do you recommend any pie? Or cake?"

"Our molten chocolate cake is my favorite. It comes with whipped cream and vanilla ice cream."

"Perfect. Do you know what you want?" Holden asked.

I grinned at him, this was exactly the kind of thing Ash, and I did. Holden matched me so perfectly that I kept waiting for the other shoe to drop, for him to reveal some gross character trait to balance the scales.

"That sounds great. Two molten chocolate cakes please."

"I feel like after 10 pm the rules of meals don't apply."

"I agree." He reached over the table for my hands again and rubbed his thumb over mine.

"I know your taste in movies. What about books?" I asked.

"Um, I will definitely disappoint you here. I only read a few books a year. It takes me forever. I am a very active guy. I prefer music."

"I listen to a lot of music, too. It really helps my creative process; I feel like music captures the mood in a really unique way."

"Do you go to a lot of concerts? That's my favorite thing to do in the summer. Festivals are a lot of fun."

"You know, I didn't really pursue that in college. But I think I would like it."

"Good. Let me take you to one this fall. We will make a weekend of it."

Ken had always shied away from making plans. He was always waiting for something better to come along. The way Holden saw me in his future without having to force it made me feel brave.

"It's a date."

While we dug into our cake, the crowd from the nearby bars started filtering in. At midnight they began karaoke in the lounge. Holden raised his eyebrows at me as we watched a very drunk college guy singing "Goodies" and trying to entice the girl he had brought. She was not impressed and promptly started pretending to text someone.

"I promise to cheer you on if you are ever moved to serenade me with Ciara," I told Holden, leaning over to steal his whipped cream.

"I will hold you to that. I am a very Ciara type of drunk."

I giggled. As we watched the dinner entertainment, I started thinking back to the last time I had done karaoke. It was with Terry, our night of country twang.

Don't turn off the music. It's so quiet when I close my eyes.

My throat tightened and all of a sudden, I wanted to cry. Maybe it wasn't right to be here. Maybe this was too soon.

"I'm actually starting to get kind of tired. Do you mind if we go?" I asked, trying to discreetly wipe my eyes.

Holden glanced over at me and concern clouded his face for a moment.

"Of course. It's getting late."

We kissed goodnight, and it blew me away as usual.

But I couldn't deny the nagging feeling that I was betraying Terry by feeling happy for even a moment when she was lying in a hospital bed.

*

True to form, Macy and I had given up on our yard long before the planting was finished. We had made a huge mess on top of it.

The forecast promised rain, so I made a point of taking the opened bags of potting soil over to the shed at the back of our yard. As I heaved in the last bag and locked the shed, I noticed that our back gate looked crooked. I stepped back and saw that the wire was pulled back as if someone had tried to pull it off and make a hole.

I shook it a little to make sure it was still secure. The shaking stirred the grass clippings on the edge of our yard, uncovering a pile of cigarette butts.

"Macy!" I called over my shoulder.

She came bounding over from the patio.

"What's up?"

I pointed to the cigarettes.

"Do you smoke?"

"Gross. No."

"How did these get here?" I asked.

If Macy wasn't sneaking outside to smoke, someone else was standing in our yard a lot. Macy suddenly grabbed my hand.

"Do you think Lucas has been here? Gina said he would be looking for her. What if he is watching the house to see if she comes here? At night we wouldn't see him this far out."

"And he's just standing here for hours?" I asked.

I tried to sound incredulous, but as soon as the words left my mouth, we both knew that's exactly what had been happening. The yard seemed very big at that moment. The fence was flimsy, and the late afternoon sky was too dark.

"Come on, let's go inside," I told Macy, putting my arm around her and leading her back inside the house so I could check the alarm system.

*

I always needed a distinct sound to every novel that I worked on. While writing my book the first time around the story seemed to pour out of me. It didn't really feel like it belonged to me and now I knew that was true.

Now that I was editing it, I struggled with how to approach the voices of the characters. Sighing I switched Spotify stations, searching for my sound. I turned the music down slightly as I heard a knock at my bedroom door. Holden poked his head inside.

"Hey, sorry. Are you working?"

I shook my head, "Not really. Come in."

I crossed my legs, and he stretched across my bed. Once again, I am struck with how well he fits into this room. When I was 11, I dreamed of being an artist and drew a series of fairies. When I tried hanging them up, I couldn't find thumbtacks, so I decided to glue them directly to the wall.

My mom freaked out, telling me that I could never remove them without destroying the paneling. I had shrugged and told her I would love them forever. When Holden first saw the drawings, he delicately took in each one. He grinned and told me that he loved trying to imagine the girl who thought fairies were sophisticated.

139

He fit in here, with my homemade drawings and posters of Ansel Adam prints. He fit in my heart as if he had been there all along.

"Did you get anything done today?"

So often people took an author's job as serious as being a circus clown. Ken had never understood, and I never let him into that part of my life. But Holden lived in that part of my life and seemed genuinely interested in watching the novel grow.

"I probably edited about two words then changed them back. I need a break."

"You didn't work, but you need a break?" he asked, smirking.

I laughed, "Yes. Exactly. You can see why I am so exhausted."

Holden stood up, "Let's take a walk. You can bounce ideas off of me."

He extended his hand. I knew he was just talking about a walk, but it always felt like so much more with him. I accepted his hand and little by little, I agreed to the rest of what was left unsaid.

*

"Add two teaspoons of garlic," I say out loud, balancing the cookbook on my arm and salivating over the photo of chicken Marsala.

I was learning to cook at my mom's level but got so hungry while cooking that I always seemed to miss the most crucial step. Macy came into the kitchen, peeking into a saucepan and grimacing slightly.

"Oh stop. This one will turn out for sure."

She raised her eyebrows playfully and sat at the island. I couldn't help but stiffen when I noticed she had my manuscript with her. She laid it on the counter and took a deep breath, deepening my suspicion.

"Did I ever tell you that before I found out about my gift, I would test out other outlets?"

I looked at her nervously.

"No. I'm sorry, I wish I would have been more open to that when I was younger. What else did you try?"

140

"Everything," she said, giggling, "Scrying, premeditation, post-meditation, telekinesis, and talking to ghosts."

"Really? How fun."

"It was. But most weren't for me. I enjoyed the ghost stuff though. I got super curious about our house and the surrounding property. I researched them in hopes of finding a sad story so I could try to connect with the ghosts by name."

I turned, my stomach feeling like it was full of lead.

"You wouldn't believe what I found out about our house," she raised her eyebrows in a challenge.

I ducked my head, "Yeah. I guess it was the inspiration for me."

She snorted, "Claire. Don't be an ass. I know."

I sat across from her, "Are you mad?"

Macy gave me a sad look, "I wish you could have told me."

I stared at my hands, "It was bad timing. I found out really recently and felt so ashamed of myself. I was such a jerk about this stuff in the past. I thought you would hate me, for not giving Mom a chance when she knew all along what was in store for me."

Macy held my hands and squeezed, "After the accident?"

I tightened my grip and tears threatened to leak out of the corners of my eyes.

"I figured. Can I hear about it now?"

I beamed at her graciousness, so thankful that she didn't have a trace of the bitterness I had accepted so willingly from Dad. I spent the next hour telling her everything.

"Len. I remember you being so sad that summer."

"I really was. I feel awful for rejecting him."

"But he was already gone, Claire. That's why you were seeing him in the first place. He died when you were 11."

"How do you know that?" I asked.

"It was all included in the article the librarian found for me. He was the person who was with Rusty that day. When he died, it was included in his obituary."

"How did he die?" I asked, not really wanting to know.

"Suicide. It really shocked the whole town."

I covered my mouth, wanting to vomit.

"Listen, I want to help you. I don't want you to shut me out of this. I think we should find Rusty's dad. Rusty getting to see him again is the only way he can move on. I think it's time the ghosts were gone from this house. We need to start over."

Chapter Eleven

Claire

Sunday dinner with Dad didn't really feel any better, but here we were again. This time I made orange chicken from a frozen dinner meal, but it was a much better option than the homemade pesto I had tried to make the night before.

"It's so nice to have my girls here," Dad said, smiling.

He was in a good mood tonight. But, the way he kept calling us his girls while completely ignoring the fact that Terry wasn't here made my stomach turn.

"It's good to be here," I said automatically.

"I have some news. More for Macy, I guess. We have a new partner at the office. His family just moved here from Chicago. I am in charge of showing him around. While getting to know him, I found out that he has a 17-year-old son who will be joining you at school in the fall. He is a very handsome young man, I thought we could set you two up. It could be fun and would definitely make them feel welcome."

I set my plate down, looking at Macy. Her face flushed and she tried to look casual.

"I don't know, Dad. I have a lot of my own stuff going on this summer."

"Do you already have a boyfriend?" he asked, confused.

Macy looked up, projecting pain. How could he know her so little? He wanted to set her up, but he didn't know if she was dating, he didn't know anything.

"No, Dad."

"Then you should give this a shot. It would really help me out at work. Team rapport, ya know? And you get to meet a nice guy in the process."

I think it was the work comment that pushed her too far. Dad wasn't involved in our lives, expecting us to make his day at work easier was a little over the top.

"I am not interested in meeting a nice guy."

"And why's that?" Dad asked, getting annoyed.

She took a deep breath, and I was so in awe of her at that moment.

"Because I have a girlfriend. Her name is Britney."

As that statement hung in the air above us, we watched Dad's face turn from pink to red, to an alarming purple.

"Did your mom put this in your head? That not only were you psychic and fucking special but that it was okay to be an idiot about your dating life? Starting this kind of rumor will follow you forever. No one will ever want you; no one will ever want you as their wife."

My mouth dropped open as Macy blushed the same awful purple.

"That's kind of the point, Dad. I don't want to be any guy's wife. And no, Mom didn't put this into my head. She wasn't a monster."

"Like hell, she wasn't. All I wanted was a normal life and look at what she left for us. Me paying two mortgages, a daughter in the hospital who is just as crazy as her mom, and a daughter who thinks she is a dike."

Macy stood up so quickly that her plate almost fell from the table.

"Screw you." As she started to leave the room, my dad stood as well, his plate actually making it to the floor and shattering.

"If you leave like this, don't ever come back."

She paused for half a second then slammed the door behind her.

I had spent the past 6 years protecting my dad, believing that he was the victim in this story. Thinking that he needed extra compassion from everyone. But I had never seen this side of him. Or maybe I was finally letting myself see this side for the first time.

My heart broke for my mom and everything she must have gone through trying to make him happy. I didn't know it was possible to hate someone you loved so much. I wondered if this was how my sisters saw me while we were growing up. I took my dad's side over and over, no matter what the argument was.

Did they see me as inflexible and judgmental? Did they see my love as conditional? This was my only chance to change who I was, to align myself with my sisters. To choose the side I should have been on from the beginning.

"If you ever speak to her like that again, you can be damn sure we will never come back. Macy is who she is, a beautiful person. She is fucking special. If you can't see that, then you will not get the privilege of being a part of our life."

Before he could respond, I stood up and joined my sister out in the car. I hugged her, spent the next hour reassuring her of my love and of how right she was in following her heart. Then we picked up Britney, and I took them both to ice cream. It felt like a night to celebrate.

*

It's been unbearably hot outside, so Holden and I had been staying in to watch movies for the last couple of days. Or rather, watching movies was the general idea, we usually ended up kissing instead.

"This movie is terrible," I said, smiling against his mouth.

"Tell me you haven't been trying to watch the movie, I am giving you my best moves here."

I laughed, but a huge bang on the front door made both of us jump. I quickly crossed the room and opened the door hesitantly, yelping a little as a bloody Gina fell through the door. I barely caught her under the armpit and went down to the ground to hold her.

"Get Macy," I said to Holden, who ran downstairs with a horrified look on his face.

Gina rolled up, trying to shut the door behind her with her foot. I leaned forward to close it for her and took canvas of her face. Her eye was turning purple with a huge gash bleeding freely underneath it; her bottom lip was torn as if her tooth went through it, and her hands were covered in cuts.

"Oh my God. Oh, my God. What happened?" I asked, horrified.

"I was at a shelter. I haven't been sleeping and I finally just passed out. He came for me. He waited until the night attendant went out for a smoke, he pulled me through the front door, and he got me into his car. I thought I was going to die," she sobbed, pulling me to her.

Holden and Macy came back into the room. Macy dropped to her knees next to me.

"Should I call the police?" she asked. "No! No! Don't, he will know I came here," Gina yelled, struggling to sit up.

"Okay, okay," Macy said soothingly, taking her hand.

"I'm going to get the first aid kit and some washcloths," Holden said, disappearing into the kitchen.

Nodding, I transferred Gina to the couch next to Macy before joining him.

"Do you know her?" Holden asked, his face white.

I sighed.

"Oh God. How do I even begin to explain this? Her name is Gina. She was one of Terry's patients, and Terry helped her escape from her abusive boyfriend."

He raised an eyebrow at me, "I feel like this isn't the whole story."

I looked at my shoes, "Do you want the whole story?"

He squeezed my hand, "Well yeah. But later, okay? Let's get her cleaned up first and figure out what to do. She should stay here. And I should probably stay the night."

I looked up, scared in more ways than one. I was happy not to have to handle this on my own but letting him help carry the burden also scared the crap out of me.

For the next hour, we cleaned Gina's wounds. They were more superficial than we initially thought. However, she definitely cracked one of her cheek bones and should have gone to the hospital. None of us could convince her so we settled on her

146

promising to stay the night so that we could file a police report in the morning.

"We have to figure out a way to keep you safe. Is there anywhere that you could go? Any family?" Macy asked, handing Gina a bowl of vegetable soup.

"No, my mom is here. She has Alzheimer's, and I am all she has left. I am taking care of her house, it will be mine someday, and I grew up in it. I can't leave, this is my home."

I took a deep breath, looking around me. As much as I hated the idea of coming back here, I couldn't imagine leaving now. This is the house my mom loved; this is where she would want me to stay.

"But, I'm tired of just letting him terrorize me. Hiding is only making him angry. I signed up for shooting lessons."

Macy's eyes widened, but I was relieved she had taken charge. I had taken shooting lessons with Ash our freshman year of college as part of their self-defense campaign. I had loved the feeling it gave me. Completely in control.

I never bought a gun, but I did feel much safer around them. I could see the appeal for someone like Gina.

"Did you buy a gun?" Holden asked, looking worried.

She shook her head, "I want to. But what if he finds it while I am trying to protect myself? What if he kills me with it?"

I tried swallowing the lump in my throat but found that I needed a drink of water to feel like I could breathe again. I wanted to help Gina but having her here made me so nervous. We had a security system, but it was old. I was glad that Holden was going to be here with us tonight.

After dinner, Gina was put to bed in Macy's room, and Macy camped out on the couch to watch a movie while talking to Britney on the phone. Mom and Terry's room were open of course, but that felt ludicrously off limits.

"Come on, let's go to bed," Holden said, extending a hand to me.

Macy wiggled her eyebrows at me, and I blushed. I brought him downstairs to my bedroom and shut the door behind us.

"Okay. So, talk. You've been distracted a lot lately, and I know it has something to do with your mom and Terry. It's more than grief. I'm here."

I took a deep breath and looked at him. This was the moment of truth. He would either believe me or he wouldn't, and I would never be able to spend time with him in good faith again.

I crossed my legs underneath me and started from the beginning. I told him about my family's history, our abilities, and how Terry's visions had led to Lucas hitting us that night.

"I saw the truck, it wasn't an accident," I ended, exhausted from talking for almost an hour.

His eyebrows furrowed and he leaned over to hold my hands.

"Claire, I am so sorry. Did you tell the police?"

"Of course. I told them about the truck, and a complaint has been filed about Lucas when he came to my sister's office to threaten her. But they ruled the crash a hit and run and never found out who the other driver was. Or, could never prove who it was. Gina came to us last week because she thinks we are in danger now; she also believes that at some point he is going to kill her. He used to want to be with her because he knew she was going to inherit everything, but I think its revenge at this point. He just wants her gone."

Holden sat back, looking serious. I knew he was trying to think of a solution. I took a deep breath, thinking that if I was going this far, I had to tell him the rest.

"Holden, Macy and I have gifts as well. Macy can see auras and sometimes gets feelings about lost items. And I... after the accident I started seeing spirits."

Holden looked up, "Well that makes sense. It runs in your family."

I laughed a little, "That makes sense? That's all you can say?"

He looked confused, "What do you want me to say?"

"That you believe me."

"I do believe you. That's what I just said."

I stood up, "It's not just that. When my dad found out about my mom, it kind of ruined their marriage. It caused a lot of problems in

148

our family. Her gift destroyed her life in a lot of ways. It's what I have been afraid of my entire life, having a gift and people not accepting me for who I am."

"Well, then your dad made a terrible mistake. He knew who she was when they got married. I am so sorry he did that to you guys. And not to make you paranoid, but there were rumors about Terry at school. She would say things to people that she couldn't possibly know about. A lot of people were kind of scared of her. But she was so sweet and being friends with CJ helped. So, this is not really a surprise."

I looked at him, searching his eyes.

"I see ghosts, Holden. It's not going to go away. This is us, my family. Me."

He stood up as well and grabbed my hands, forcing me to look at him.

"Stop trying to push me away. I said that I believe you. I accept you. I accept all of you. I am not your dad."

Despite myself, I believed him. Tears filled my eyes as I let him hold me. I trusted him when he told me that he loved me. He stayed with me all night.

*

"Are you sure that you can handle this?" Macy asked.

She was holding my hand as we made our way to the dock. We arrived, I busied myself with laying down a blanket. It was a little past 11, and the ground was already damp from the dew.

"No, I am not. But I have to be. Caroline's story needs to be told so I can figure out how to help her move on. I want it to be here, our house can't take any more of her pain. It has to end here."

Macy sat down and lit a white candle. I raised my eyebrow in question.

"For light?"

"For positivity. White candle light is supposed to surround us in warmth to keep out anything bad."

Goosebumps broke out on my arms.

"I know that opening this door is risky. But this is the only way that I know how to make things better."

I believed that, but the darkness made this more real than ever. Macy held my hand, afraid.

"I wish Mom were here. She would know how I am supposed to protect myself, the right way to do this."

"Maybe you will have a chance to ask her someday."

"Mac, I want to try something, but I feel like I need to ask for your permission. We are going to hold hands while I try to bring Caroline here. I wanted to know if it was okay if I tried to share my gift with you, to see if that is possible."

Her eyes clouded with fear, but she set her jaw firmly and agreed. I squeezed her hand then closed my eyes.

I called to my mind the scene in my book where Caroline dies. I called her, from the house, from the darkness, from all of her hiding places. After a few minutes, I felt the air still and knew that she was here.

Macy felt it too and stiffened.

"Caroline?" I asked quietly.

"Yes," she whispered back.

Macy jumped, and I open my eyes. Caroline was standing right behind her.

"Are you ready Mac? She is right behind you. I don't want you to be scared."

She nodded, still closing her eyes. I stared at Caroline, opening myself up to what she is made of and how the cold wind feels on my skin. After a few minutes, Macy sat up straighter.

"I can hear her. Her breath is on my shoulders, and I smell the lake water. It's okay, but I am not going to open my eyes yet."

"That's okay, thank you for going with me."

Holding my concentration to project and receive at the same time was difficult, but something inside of me was growing. Getting stronger.

"Why are we here?" Caroline asked.

"So that you can move on. I know that you died here, but I also know that isn't the whole story. You are keeping something from me. And until I know what that is, I can't help you, which means I can't help Rusty."

She closed her eyes.

"But I am so ashamed."

"Of what?"

When Caroline opened her eyes, they are glowing like hot coals.

"You won't tell him the truth? You will just help him?"

Before I am done answering her, that whining noise is back, and I reel as she filled me with memories. Memories that are hot with pain and dripping with murky pond water.

A bloodcurdling scream ripped me from the arms of my lover, and I ran outside to where the boys were swimming in our pool. Len ran around the backyard, his face a waxy yellow and his eyes bulging.

"What happened?" I screamed.

Lens father held onto his son's shoulders, his shirt was still off, and he looked like he was ready to run.

"We tried to make a rope swing, we thought we could climb onto the clubhouse and use the rope to swing into the pool. But the rope got tangled, and Rusty tried to fix it," Len yelled, nearly belligerent with fear.

I nodded my head, not understanding. Len shook crazily and lifted a spastic hand up to point at the tree next to the clubhouse.

Rusty hung from the tree with the rope twisted around his slender neck. His eyes looked out lifelessly, and his skin was already deepening into a deathly purple. It was like something out of a horror movie.

My body began to shake violently, and I walked across the yard like I was moving through sand. I kept thinking that if I got to him soon enough, he would begin to breathe. If I reached him in time, I could rewind this entire day.

Fear flooded my body. I somehow climbed onto the clubhouse roof and had to reach for my still swinging son, holding him and trying to untangle the rope from his body. Lens father joined me and used his pocket knife to cut him down. As the rope became slack his wet swimming trunks ripped from my hands, and he fell to the ground, his leg contorting beneath him.

I made it to the ground, swaying with nausea. I was sick. Rusty was so still. I folded over him and listened to his chest. Silence never hurt me as badly as it did at that moment.

I began doing compressions and giving him mouth to mouth. I tried to remember life guard training from my teen days. But it was no use. I compressed his chest and heard a small crack. I ripped my hands back, whimpering.

My beautiful little boy was broken... He was gone because I wasn't here to watch him. I had killed my son. Len screamed over and over, running around the yard manically.

"We have to call the police," Len's father yelled down at me.

But I am a million miles away.

Five minutes ago, I was in my lover's arms. Ignoring the world and thinking that my pain was the biggest thing in the world. I had no idea.

I thought that things were going to be better. He and I were going to start over, in a place that was sunny all the time, where Rusty and Len would play in the sand and be the brothers, they always wished they were.

But now... Rusty was gone, I should have been watching. I had no idea about pain. Slowly I picked him up and walked over to the car. I couldn't go to the hospital; I couldn't explain this to my husband. I can't face the world after... this. I didn't want to live without my son.

"What are you doing?" my lover yelled.

Ignoring him I gently buckled Rusty into his booster chair and slid into the driver's seat. It wasn't too late. We could still go somewhere beautiful together, one last time. As I pulled out of the driveway, my love chased after us, almost catching the door handle before falling.

I began to sob as I drove down our block. I remembered driving down this same block on our way home from the hospital, Rusty a tiny swaddled bundle in the back seat. This is the block where he took his first steps, where he learned to ride his bike, where we went to the block party where he met Len.

The sleepovers where I met his father. One conversation led to a thousand more, and a three-year affair. To a love that felt so wrong and somehow also like the rightest thing in the world. But I was selfish.

A mother shouldn't put her own needs above the needs of her child. And Rusty needed me to be present. He was the one who suffered most of all. As I pressed on the gas and aimed towards the pond dock, I rested my hand on my stomach.

Well, maybe not most of all. I am sorry little one. This is for the best.

Our car was weightless for just one second then hit the water. I never imagined that the water could feel so much like concrete. My head slammed against the steering wheel, and my eyes swam. I never thought that I could bleed that much in that little amount of time. But the darkness came quickly, and I drifted away.

I choked, trying to swallow the marshy taste in my mouth and grabbing onto Macy. She leaned forward to whack me on the back, looking worried. Her face was white, and I wondered how much of the connection I had kept. Caroline was now sitting, rocking with her knees drawn up to her chest.

"She was pregnant," I said to Macy.

My eyes watered, and my throat still burned with water. Macy's white face told me that she had seen way more than she wanted.

"I couldn't have moved on. I couldn't have gone through with our plan, to raise my baby with Len's father after Rusty was gone. This was my punishment," Caroline said.

I understood why she was so fractured. It wasn't just her spirit. She was responsible for the death of her unborn baby. For that reason alone, her spirit would always be broken. She would get no peace.

But it wasn't only that. I suddenly remembered Rusty taking me here, him feeling like this place was important to his story.

153

Macy clenched my hand, before free falling back into the memories. I saw her eyes film over slightly, seeing my vision reflecting in her eyes.

The cold water startled me. My legs were wet, and my eyelids were glued shut. Using my hands, I forced them open. I felt like I was looking out of the kaleidoscope that Daddy got me for my birthday. I was on top of the clubhouse, we had been trying to tie a rope to our tree to swing into the pool. I jumped, and kind of flew before coming down hard.

My throat throbbed angrily, and I was having trouble breathing. But now I was in the car. Mommy was in the front seat, laying on the steering wheel like she was taking a nap.

"Mommy?" I called out, the scream of my throat bringing tears to my eyes.

When I tried to reach forward to her, an intense pain shot down my side. I reached down gently and screamed when I saw that a little piece of my bone had escaped from my leg. I hated seeing it in the world like that, it was supposed to be hidden by my skin.

"Mommy, my leg. Why is it like this?" I looked forward, really seeing the front seat for the first time.

We were in the pond. Why were we in the pond? The big front window of the car was broken like a spider web.

"Mommy! Why are we here? We're in the pond. The water is getting in. Stop it, stop it right now."

The water was up to my thigh, and Mommy was still sleeping. Was she sleeping? Our car was broken. Was she broken? Is that why she wasn't answering?

"Mommy," I said softly, looking down at my leg again.

I tried my seat belt, but it was frozen in the water, not budging at all. Daddy usually helped me unbuckle; I was better at pushing it in.

"I'm stuck," I gasped.

My breaths were cutting the inside of my chest. The water was up to my belly button. The car was broken. Mommy was broken. I was going to be broken too.

I leaned forward, dissolving. Macy was hysterical, she shouldn't have seen that. It was too much.

"Caroline, you have to leave. Until you move on Rusty will be stuck here forever, looking for you and being so lonely. He has been so scared and alone," I say, letting myself cry freely.

Caroline shook her head, "I can't."

"You have to, he wasn't dead. He was unconscious, his neck didn't break. He was still alive when you buckled him into that car seat. You panicked. You decided to commit suicide, and when you were passed out, he woke up. He drowned. You killed your baby, and you killed Rusty too."

I was filled with such a deep hatred for her. I wanted her gone, I wanted to run home to find Rusty. To hug him and try to make his hurt a little less profound.

"If you really love Rusty at all, do this for him. Let him move on."

Caroline cried for a few more minutes then looked up.

"It will really help him?"

I bowed my head, having to choke down my anger. She didn't deserve his forgiveness; he had wandered alone for years because of her.

"Yes. It's the only way he is going to be able to cross over."

Caroline stood and looked out to the pond for a minute.

"I'm afraid."

"Why?" I asked, following her gaze out over the water and the huge moon it reflected back into the sky.

"Because I have seen the siren that's waiting for me. And it's not heaven."

The hairs on the back of my neck stood up as Caroline turned to face me. She took a deep breath, steadying herself, then the whining noise became so loud Macy and I both had to cover our ears.

But I saw it through to the end. Her eyes glowed that ember red until it seemed to devour her whole body, and then she was gone. She had left by fire, but all that was left was the coldest I have ever felt.

I thought that helping my first ghost move on would help me communicate with my mom and I missed her more than I ever thought possible. I came home terrified and freezing,

After a hot shower and full nights rest, I felt like I was finally getting a handle on all of this. I spent the following morning in my mom's room, meditating on her bed and reaching out to her with everything I had. After three hours it was so still that it was like a personal slight.

I cried for me, for everything I put my mom through while she was here, and for what the future held in store for me. If I didn't have her here, I didn't want any part of this gift. With my eyes blurry I began pulling myself to the edge of the bed.

The sun seemed to move behind the curtains, and the room was cast in darkness. I ran my hand across my face and then froze with my arm still in the air. It wasn't the sun.

Three solid figures stood at the opposite wall. They blended in with the afternoon shadows but were deeper than any darkness I had ever experienced. The tops of their bodies melded into the wall, but their legs were separate and clear.

"Caroline?" I choked out.

One of the figures pulled away from the wall and solidified into a human shape. They slowly glided across the carpet and stopped at the edge of the bed where I had pulled myself. I could feel pain radiating from it. Screams tore into my ears, and I was filled with such bottomless emptiness. Part of me wanted to fall into it and see if I could find my mom that way.

"Mom?" I whispered, leaning forward.

The air seemed to freeze as I got closer and closer to touching the wispy black air in front of me. Suddenly I heard a huge crack of energy and fell forward, hitting the carpet without catching myself.

When I looked up, the shadow figures were gone. Caroline was gone, she had never been this darkness. I had let it in somehow, and it was hell-bent on taking me with it.

I was so used to relationships being for show, as a way for Ken to get attention and sometimes even pick up other girls. But when Holden kissed me, it was because he wanted me. It was impossible not to get lost in.

"Right now, the moonlight is turning your hair almost red. You really are just, gorgeous," he told me, holding my cheek.

I basked in his smile as he leaned in to kiss me. We had been dancing at a new bar for the last hour, and I never wanted it to end.

My phone started vibrating, and I reluctantly pulled it from my jeans pocket. It was a hospital phone number. A number I memorized since a nurse was kind enough to give me weekly updates on Terry.

But it was 11:30 pm. An update made no sense unless it was the worst of news. With trembling hands, I answered the phone.

"Hello?"

"Claire?"

It was Macy. She was bawling. I sunk into a chair next to the dance floor. A part of me was relieved, if she was able to call me, then she was okay. If she was calling me, then Terry was still alive.

"Macy, what happened? What are you doing at the hospital?"

"Britney and I came home, and someone was waiting for us. He tried to hurt me, and Britney wouldn't let him. She's in the hospital."

*

Running through the emergency room doors held a particular kind of déjà vu for me. I wondered if this was how Macy felt, confused and guilty.

I was escorted to Britney's room, and Macy was silently sobbing in a chair near her bed. Her cheek was bruised, and her hands seemed bloody. I kneeled next to her chair.

"What happened? You said someone was waiting for you?"

She jerked her head yes, sobbing harder.

"I unlocked the gate, and he was hiding in the dark porch. He hit me from behind. I don't think he saw Britney. She still was carrying her laptop bag and swung it at him. He punched her and started kicking her on the ground. It was awful. I was screaming and trying to push him away. Finally, one of the neighbors must have heard. He ran when he heard the police sirens."

"Did you see who it was?"

"No, it was dark. Where were you?" she asked, leaning away so I couldn't hug her.

I looked at my hands, "I was with Holden. I left a note in the kitchen."

Macy glared at me, "A note in the kitchen didn't keep me from coming home to a house he knew was empty. You should have been there."

"Macy," I tried to hold her hand.

She snatched it away and turned from me.

"I'll see you at home. I am going to stay with Britney tonight."

I stood up stiffly. I was apparently dismissed. As I drove myself home that night, I wondered if this was my cost, the cost that Terry warned me about. I was falling for Holden, every time I saw him, I could feel myself plunging into a love I had never experienced before.

But loving him had left Macy in a position that could have killed her. Maybe it was time to make a choice.

*

When Holden came over for dinner the next week, I was overwhelmed with emotion and on edge. Britney was all right and was let out of the hospital the day before. But things were still strained between Macy and me.

I was trying to be home every night in case she needed me, but it didn't seem to be helping.

"Where's Macy tonight?" Holden asked, serving my plate of chicken and rice pilaf first.

"She and Britney went to a movie and then are going to a friend's house."

He wiggled his eyebrows at me, "Oh sweet. We have the house to ourselves."

I blushed and tried to roll my eyes. Our kisses good night were leading to a place where it would be hard to say no. And I wasn't sure I wanted to say no. When I was with Holden, I felt so safe and at peace that I craved him more than anything.

At the same time, I couldn't deny that I hated wanting him here because it gave him the option of leaving and breaking my heart. It took my attention away from my sister and for what payoff?

We ate dinner quietly and then decided to watch a movie in the living room.

"I brought Terry flowers today," Holden told me, knitting his fingers in mine.

Thinking of my sister and of my mom sent my stomach boiling. I recoiled away from him, tucking my hand under my leg instead.

"What's wrong?" he asked.

"You didn't even know Terry. Why would out do that?"

"Aside from her being important to you? She is there because she tried to protect someone. I respect her, even if we haven't talked since high school."

I looked at him, suddenly wanting to fight. Terry being there wasn't fair, my mom being gone wasn't fair, me having to take care of Macy on my own wasn't fair.

Holden had no idea what that was like. He couldn't come into the game this late and expect to be part of everything. He couldn't wait for me to put him above my family.

"Do you think that gets you points? That if you bring my comatose sister flowers that it guarantees you will get into my pants?"

Holden sat up, his face red, "Are you kidding me? When have I ever treated you like a conquest?"

"What about back in the kitchen? You implied that because Macy wasn't here, we were going to have sex."

"I was joking! What is your problem? You've been picking a fight all night."

"What's my problem? Besides my mom being dead and my whole family falling apart? How about people jumping my sister while I am out on a date with you? I have more on my plate than this relationship believe it or not."

He sat forward, "You know. I am not going to go here with you. This isn't about me, or us. This is about you. Do you want me to leave so you can get ahold of yourself?"

I sat back, pissed that he was going to leave instead of talking this out with me. This was about us. I had more to deal with than Holden, he should have understood that.

"No. I want you to leave. Period. I need to be here for my sister. You're a distraction."

His eyebrows raised and for a second, I saw hurt in his eyes, which affected me more than I wanted it to. He stood up, grabbed his coat, and left. I wanted to feel victorious, but all I felt was empty.

*

It had taken a month of emailing and convincing, but Rusty's dad was finally here.

I had told him the whole story. Knowing his son when I was younger and being able to communicate with him. I wasn't sure if he really believed me, but he would give anything for a chance to say goodbye.

Rusty's father had remarried and had a daughter. Picking this back up would be the most painful thing in his life since losing Rusty and his wife. But when I told him that it would help Rusty move on, he couldn't say no.

After an awkward cup of coffee, I looked out the window to see Rusty walking out of the open clubhouse door. It was now or never.

"I'm sorry if this is hard for you, but he's here. This is still his favorite place to play," I told Rusty's father.

I stood up and led him out to the clubhouse. He shook his head.

"No, this place never turned sad for me. We built this club house together. We used to camp out there in the summer and then fish in the morning. After the... Accident, I restored it so that other kids could experience it."

"Thank you. I played in that club house almost every day until I was 13."

I stopped and looked at Rusty, who was lingering in the doorway. I couldn't read his expression, but his glow subtlety grew.

"Rusty? Do you want to come over?" I asked, feeling a little self-conscious talking to him in front of Russell.

Rusty looked suspicious at us but clambered over and plopped down on the ground at our feet.

"He's sitting," I explained, joining Rusty on the ground.

Russell hesitated for a moment before joining us as well.

"He looks so... old," Rusty said finally.

I laughed, "He tells me you look old."

Russell smiled, his resolve fading.

"But his smile is the same. Is he happy?"

I turned to him, "He wants to know if you are happy. You can go ahead and talk to him. He hears you."

Russell took that in but seemed to need to gather what he wanted to say.

"It took a long time, but yes, I am happy. I got remarried. She is a lovely lady named Christine and last year we had a baby named..."

"Charlotte," Rusty and Russell said together.

"How did you know," I asked Rusty.

"Charlotte's Web is my favorite book. I always wanted a little sister so we could name her that."

"He says he always wanted to name a baby sister Charlotte."

Russell's eyes widened, and I could see that he actually believed me for the first time.

"I know. If it was a boy, we were going to name him Charlie Rusty. Even though you are gone, you are a part our life every single day."

My eyes teared up as I watched him stop talking to me and fill his son in on his life over the past three years. Rusty listened, smiling, and getting brighter by the minute.

"What does he need from me?" Russell asked, wiping his eyes.

I looked at Rusty.

"I don't need anything for me. I am happy he has a baby to love, he was such a good dad. Ask him to promise that he will read to her every night, that she will grow up with stories about her brother Rusty, that he will take her fishing and show her the photo of that huge bass I caught that summer. That he will teach her our good night song and hug her for me every single day."

As I relayed that, Russell grinned, crying even harder.

"Of course, buddy. But I won't have to change a thing. Last night we read A Monster at the End of this book, I told her about the time you hid peas under the couch cushions. I took her fishing in April, and she helped me reel in the biggest trout ever. She sings your good night song every night and kisses the photo of you that we have on her nightstand. She loves you Rusty boy, almost as much as me."

Rusty stood, touching his dad's cheek. Russell's eyes got huge before he gently touched his cheek and leaned into it, closing his eyes. Rusty glowed until I almost wanted to shield my eyes. There was warmth and love in that light, I bathed in it. And then he was gone.

*

"Does this look okay?" Macy asked, spinning in a light pink sundress with strappy sandals.

"Gorgeous, where are you guys going tonight?" I asked, closing my laptop where I was outlining my second book.

"To a party for pep squad. Getting to know the girls and such. Are you and Holden hanging out tonight?"

I wrung my hands, "Actually. We aren't really hanging out anymore."

She gaped at me before sitting on the couch beside me.

"Why? What happened?"

"You got hurt. Britney was injured. I need to focus on being here for you."

Macy sighed.

"Claire when I said that… In the hospital. I was upset. I missed Mom. That's not what I meant at all."

"But that doesn't keep it from being true. I have more responsibilities than he does. This is where I need to be."

Macy leaned back against the couch.

"I told you that your auras matched perfectly, right?"

"Yeah."

"Mom and Dads did, too."

I laughed, "That kind of proves my point. They weren't meant to end up together."

She leaned forward and held my hand.

"That's not the point. The point is that they were supposed to be part of each other's story. They were together so that we could exist. I know this, it's part of my gift. They were meant for each other for that chapter in their life. I also know that Holden is part of your destiny. Nothing is permanent, life isn't permanent. But Mom and Terry would love him. They would like seeing you happy and would want to be part of this chapter in your life."

Tears filled my eyes, and I tried to brush them away.

"I think I messed things up, Mac."

"Do you love him?" she asked.

I realized that we had never actually talked like this before. I never let her into my dating life or let her see this vulnerable side of myself. It was scary, but how I felt was even scarier. I loved him so much I felt like I was swallowed up in it.

"I have never felt like this about anyone else in my entire life. He makes me a better person, and it's easy to imagine a future with him. But how could he forgive me? I told him that he was nothing more than a distraction. I ruined everything."

She shook her head, "No. I don't think so. Your auras match perfectly, Claire. But love is about so much more than that. It's about being there for each other; it's about loving them even when it's not easy."

"Kind of like loving your sister even though she is not always easy to love?" I asked, blushing a little.

"You are easier to love than you think. Maybe you need to work on loving yourself first."

I laughed and hugged her, "When did you get so smart about this kind of stuff?"

"It's a gift."

Chapter Twelve

Claire

I knew that I really only had one more chance to make myself clear. I also knew that I was terrible at talking about emotions and that this was going to be horrifying and might ruin my chances altogether.

Holden was stocking groceries at check stand four, smiling at an older woman and offering to bring her cart out for her. As she told him no, he watched her leave the store to make sure.

His eyes caught mine as I stood by the automatic doors. I smiled, but my heart fell as he forced his eyes away from mine. There was no one else in line, so I joined him at the end of the checkout stand, knowing the cashier was staring at us.

"Hey, can we talk?" I said quietly, hating how red his face was and that I made him that uncomfortable.

"You have time for me now?" he asked, refusing to look at me.

I looked down. This was already terrible. I was losing my nerve by the second.

"Do you want me to leave?"

Holden finally looked at me, and I saw the hurt in his eyes, which was worse than the anger.

"No, I have a minute. But I already took my lunch, so you have to make it quick."

I nodded and followed him to the back of the store into a hallway where the employee bathrooms were located.

"What?" he said, shoving his hands into his apron.

I looked around, wondering where to start.

"So... you know how pots have lids that seem to fit them perfectly?" I said quickly, blushing furiously.

His mouth dropped open; I had no idea where the pot metaphor had come from. It seemed to knock him off his guard, and he almost laughed.

"Pots? You ignored me for a week and then came to my work, to talk about pots?" he said, shoving his smile away.

"Not just pots, their lids…."

He sighed and started to walk away. I grabbed his hand. Gasping, I clenched his fingers as electricity seemed to flow between us. He jumped like I hurt him but looked back and stopped walking.

"Please listen." I took a deep breath and stared at my shoes, "So pots come in all shapes and sizes and are sold with these lids that fit them perfectly. And you bring this pot home and kind of take it for granted because it's always done its job and made you happy. But then one day you lose the lid, and the pot is kind of useless on its own. The pot just sits in the cupboard and has to realize that they should have appreciated their lid because it makes them complete."

As my speech ended the silence in the room seemed to take on a life of its own and thicken until I was suffocating. Finally, Holden's hand found my chin, and he guided my face to look into his.

"Claire. What the hell are you talking about?" he said, fully smiling now.

My eyes filled with tears. Why was this so difficult for me? I was a writer.

"Isn't it obvious?! I had you, and we fit perfectly. But then I was selfish and thought I didn't need to belong to a set. And now I am just some lonely pot sitting on a shelf all by myself wishing I had my lid back. Because a pot and lid's love are extraordinary and I want to be a part of it."

Holden laughed and had to step away to keep from falling over.

"Okay, I'm sorry. I'll go."

I tried to step around him as I wiped my cheeks. I could never shop here again, which broke my heart even more because it was the only local grocery store that sold my favorite ice cream.

"No, no. Please don't," Holden gasped in between his manic giggles.

I stopped but didn't want to look behind me to see his laughing. I was horrified enough. He grabbed my hand and stepped in front of me. His face was flushed, and he had the most amazing grin on his face that I had ever seen.

"You being this lonely pot is quite the problem."

"Shut up," I said, trying to push him away.

As I pushed his chest, he grabbed my shoulder and brought me closer. With one swoop I was in his arms, and his lips were on mine. Nothing else mattered.

It was a kiss I had avoided for my whole life. It was a kiss that shattered every other kiss and left them forgotten. It was a kiss that consumed me and turned a new chapter in the book that was my life.

"Okay. That was nice," I breathed once we stepped back.

Holden looked into my eyes seriously and held my face in his hands, "Claire. I promise to be your lid forever. You will never be alone ever again."

It was the worst speech of my life, the longest five minutes that I have ever had the pleasure of inflicting on myself. But it had led me here, to being accepted as the freak that I was. To being received as a set, a pot and lid that would never lose each other again.

*

"I'm saying that we both live here, I should be able to cook too," Macy said.

She led the way into the kitchen and dropped her groceries on the counter.

"That sounds a lot like you don't like the way I make mac and cheese."

"You are so right about that. Use some milk! If it's not creamy, it's not mac and cheese."

"Mac! Do you know what's in that cheese packet? Death, its poison."

She laughed and headed into the living room.

"I am not having this conversation with you again."

I shook my head but smiled. I grabbed the pasta out of the bags and headed to the pantry. I opened the door and leaned in to place them on the shelf.

I smelled the chemicals on the rag before I was aware of the man holding it.

*

My eyes felt like sand was trapped under the lids, and I tried to lift my hands to rub them. They refused to move, and I struggled where I sat.

Eventually, I was able to open them enough to see that we weren't in my kitchen anymore. I was tied to a chair, and Macy was sitting across from me, she was sobbing quietly.

"Mac," I gurgled, tasting my own blood and feeling like I had cotton shoved into my cheeks.

"Claire, try not to move. Please," she begged, gesturing with her head to the doorway.

A tall man was in a living room, pacing while spinning around a pocket knife. Panic blossomed through my limbs, creating webs of pain. I looked down at myself. Blood was everywhere.

"What happened?" I whispered.

Macy started sobbing quietly, not wanting to look at me.

"I came to first and tried to struggle free. You were laying on the ground still unconscious…. He beat you. He beat you while you laid there. I heard bones cracking. He told me that if I fought him again, he would tear you apart."

My stomach rolled. I felt dirty from the inside out. What if Macy hadn't been awake? Would he have stopped at hitting a lifeless body? What did he want with us?

As if reading my thoughts, he looked over and noticed that I was awake.

"Good morning, sunshine. How does your face feel?"

I glared as he smirked down at me.

"That was a warning. You try to get free; you won't get far."

"Why are we here? Who are you?" I asked.

"That's right, you don't know me. But you know Gina. You've helped Gina. And there are consequences for girls who don't know their place."

He slapped duct tape over my mouth and then did the same to Macy. My nose was so swollen that I could barely breathe. It started to sink in that I might not leave this house alive. I heard the front door creak as a key is slid into the lock.

He raised his eyebrows as if to say, *show time*, and stepped into the kitchen to hide.

I heard footsteps through the living room, and Gina stepped into the kitchen.

She dropped her purse, her mouth gaping in fear. She rushed to me and ripped the tape off of my mouth before noticing the man leaning against a counter casually. The skin from lips stung and I tasted blood in my mouth again.

"Where have you been?" he asked, choking Gina from behind and bringing the knife to her side.

She whimpered, "Please, Lucas. This is crazy. Why are they here?"

Lucas? The psycho that killed my mom? My stomach contorted and I felt vomit curling up into my throat. He spun her around and used the back of his hand to send her flying into the dining room table.

"You need to be taught a few things. Don't question me ever again. They are here because you made them part of this. I thought after Terry you would have learned your lesson."

Gina sunk to the ground. She looked from Lucas to us, seeming to sink into herself. Her shoulders finally slumped, and with them, all of my hope evaporated. She was weak, he knew that. He was in control now.

Lucas took in her resignation and walked over to me, pushing my chair into the table like I was a guest.

"Gin, honey. It's getting late. Why don't you fix us up some dinner," he said, his voice hard.

He walked around to the other side of the room and sat Macy at the table as well before sitting next to her. He took Macy's bound hands and laid them on the polka dot placemat, holding his knife above them.

"No!" I screamed.

Lucas laughed, "I don't think you get how this works yet."

"Don't hurt her. Do whatever you want to me, but please don't hurt my baby sister," I pleaded, sobbing even harder.

Macy shook her head, but I tried not to make eye contact with her. Lucas put my hands on the table as well.

"What's it going to be, Gina? Meatloaf or fried chicken?"

He swung the knife back and forth before plunging it into my wrist. The noise that tore from me was ungodly. It was the same wrist that I had broken only months before. The new delicate bone had been severed completely.

Gina scrambled to her feet, glancing in my direction with dead eyes. I hated her so much at that moment. Lucas left the knife in, and I tried to breathe through the pain.

Over the next hour, Gina cooked. Lucas forced her to banter with him like they were on a date, completely ignoring us. She put four plates on the table and served us, even Macy, who still wore tape on her mouth. Lucas took one bite of the meatloaf and smiled at Gina.

"Good girl. My favorite."

She relaxed a little and sat next to me, refusing to look at my still bleeding wrist.

"I'm glad you like it," she stuttered.

"I have been meaning to ask you. How do you feel about fall weddings? We could take a trip up to Niagara Falls next month and be hitched by Thanksgiving."

Gina looked around with her empty eyes, seeming to not know where she was.

"Hitched? But... I thought we were waiting."

Lucas sat his fork down, "Why would we wait?"

"Terry thought we should go to counseling together... to work through our issues before anything became... official."

170

I watched him flush in slow motion, starting at his hands and going all the way up to his forehead. He leaned in and ripped the knife from my arm. I saw black spots and reeled forward.

Lucas stood so quickly he knocked his chair back and stormed over to Gina. He ripped her backward by the hair and put the knife to her throat.

"After all of this, you still don't get it. We are getting married. You are mine. You always have been."

Tears leaked out of her eyes.

"Lucas, please." He smashed her face into the table, screaming.

"Please! Please! That's all you can say. You keep asking me, but what about what I am asking of you? I only want you to obey me! Love me! Why is that so hard?"

Gina tried to stand up, and Luke wrapped one arm around her shoulders, dragging her into the living room.

"Well, I love you. And I'm going to prove it."

I watched him drag her across the hardwood onto a carpet, where he dropped her. He took off his shirt then climbed on top of her. When she realized what was happening, she started to scream, rolling side to side and attempting to kick him.

I closed my eyes, not wanting to witness a rape before dying myself. I pulled my hands into my lap, and the rope slipped over them. My broken wrist made them loose, and the blood made the rope slippery.

Biting my lip, I folded my hand in half and slid it out of the ropes. Macy's eyes widened, and she shook her head ferociously. She didn't want me to get hurt, but this was my moment. This was my only shot at saving her life. To do something right.

I quickly leaned down and untied my ankles. I stood and walked across the kitchen quietly, over to where a phone hung on the wall. Lucas had gotten Gina's skirt hiked up as they fought. He ripped her panties and was struggling to unbutton his jeans while keeping one hand on her neck.

As I reached the wall, I saw that Gina's purse was still on the floor. Something silver winked out at me. Her gun.

Lucas had murdered my mom and put my sister in the hospital. He meant to kill us.

What if I could end this right now? I dialed 911 and left the phone on the counter. Hopefully, that would be enough. But I hoped they took their time.

"Lucas, get away from her," I said, pointing the gun at him and trying to keep my hands from shaking.

He turned around, shocked but still half crazed. In one motion he held the knife to Gina's throat.

"Don't be a hero, Claire. Heroes still get innocent blood on their hands."

I looked from Gina's eyes to Lucas over and over, I heard Macy thrashing in the kitchen. I thought of my mom and how disappointed she already was in me. And I couldn't.

One second of hesitation was all he needed. Lucas tore to his feet and punched me square in the jaw. The gun dropped out of my slick hands, and I started to fall.

Gina jumped on Lucas's back, hitting him with her fists and bawling.

"I hate you," she cried in a watery voice.

Lucas threw her down but lost his knife. It scuttled to my feet, and I picked it up. I couldn't reach the gun but kicked forward with my remaining strength. The gun skittered towards Gina, and she scrambled for it.

She picked it up quickly and aimed it at Lucas. He laughed, standing above us.

"You still don't get it. You can't just shoot me."

Gina looked at me. He was right, we could call the police. In my panic, I remembered that I already had. But something inside of me hoped that they were too late. This had to end tonight.

"Gina, he will never stop. He will get out of jail, and he will murder every last one of us. Look at yourself! It's time to be strong."

She looked down at her skirt, the blood on her thighs and her bruised forearms.

"I think you're the one who doesn't get it," she whispered to Lucas.

Then she pulled the trigger. Even though I thought it was what I wanted, it startled me. I heard Macy kicking in the kitchen and rose to help her.

Gina sank to her knees, still holding the gun out in front of her. I held her up and trying not to sob.

"You saved us, Gina. You saved us. You're free."

Her eyes spun crazily before finding my face, "I had to. He was going to kill us. I had to, right?"

I nodded, already unsure of myself. A dead man was behind us. I would never get the image of her shooting him out of my head. She repeated, "I'm free," over and over but was also shaking her head no. He was gone, but he was still very real to Gina.

She was never going to feel free. Lucas was going to follow her in her dreams forever. He might make a few appearances in mine as well.

*

I tried looking at my phone as discreetly as possible, but Holden caught me and raised his eyebrows.

"Okay, okay," I said laughing, putting my phone in my purse.

It had been two weeks since the shooting, but I was still nervous about leaving Macy at home. She had all but pushed me out the door for my first date with Holden since everything happened.

He had gone all out. We ate at the best Mexican restaurant in town, went ice skating, and now we were sharing ice cream cones and watching the last baseball game of our team's season. I was completely exhausted.

"She's okay. Do you think she is sitting at home missing you? Or feeling afraid? She probably called Britney the moment you left and is getting into some trouble of her own."

I blushed, "That makes me want to check on her for an entirely different reason."

He laughed and kissed my cheek.

173

As the game ended Holden drove me home, and we lingered in the car, kissing like we were 16. I had never fallen this fast, but at the same time, every single part of it was natural and right.

After finding out what happened, Holden rushed to the hospital and stayed with me until we were released. He stayed the night with us, staying on the couch and holding me when I had nightmares. He had flowers sent to our house, for Macy and me both.

For a full week until our dining room was filled with roses, daisies, and lilies. More than that, he left my flowers with books and notes with how they tied in. Roses for Alice's Adventures in Wonderland. A pressed flower for the Girl with the Dragon Tattoo. Poppies for the Wizard of Oz. The last flowers were lilacs because they represented everlasting childhood. He wrote that they were for my upcoming book because in that way Rusty would always have a happy ending.

When I kissed him, I wished on forever.

"Are you tired? Did our date tucker you out?" I asked, looking at my hands.

"Um, not really. Why? Are you in the mood to go out for a beer?" Holden asked.

I looked at him, wanting to see his face.

"No, I thought maybe you could come inside. I have beer, and we could have a nightcap, here. In my room. Where you stay. All night."

He laughed, "I want to make sure I am not assuming anything here because that's super rude. But are you asking me to sleep over?"

I smiled, "I am not asking you to sleep anywhere, but I am asking you to stay."

Holden grinned, turned off the engine, and went around the car to open my door. He extended his hand to me and kissed the back of it before leading me into the house.

*

I could hear Macy giggling on the phone, Holden was fast asleep in my bed, and the house felt full for the first time since I moved back in. I didn't want to sleep, not tonight. I wanted this feeling to last forever.

I went into my new office, the other half of the den, and started to unload my books and folders. I had a brand-new book outlined, and my first book was going to be published soon. Just as I was putting my bookshelf together, a whoosh of warmth swirled around me.

I stilled, knowing she was here but almost unable to turn around. Her hand covered mine, and when I saw the amethyst ring, she always wore, I broke down.

"Mom," I whispered, leaning my head against the shelf.

I turned, and my first thought was that she was more beautiful than I remembered.

"My Claire."

I sank down, staring at her. I had wished for her for months, but now everything I wanted to say left me completely. She sat in front of me, the smile never leaving her face.

"Are you safe?" I asked, unsure of what I meant by that.

She sighed with contentedness.

"Of course. It's beautiful and bright here. Everything we ever dreamed of and more."

Tears streamed down my cheeks, and I just basked in her glow.

"A little boy came to me. He told me you were ready. I am so proud of you, Claire. I always have been."

"I know. I know you were."

She grinned and leaned forward.

"Tell me your news."

I thought of how many times she had dreamed of this moment and wished more than anything it could have happened while she was still here.

"My gift. I can see ghosts, Mom. I helped two this summer alone. It's hard, but it's right."

"No, sweetheart. Not that gift. Your first gift, your writing. Tell me about your book."

175

My mouth dropped open a little, and I realized this wasn't her dream. She didn't want me to tell her that she was right, I didn't owe her anything. Maybe it was never her dream. But this moment, her wanting to be a part of my world, it was mine. She had seen me all along.

"It's called Sneakers in the Water...."

Chapter Thirteen

Terry

September 2015

Physical therapy was hard but so much more satisfying than I ever imagined. I was getting stronger, but it was slow work.

CJ was there every single day, helping me feed myself and then holding my hand as I took my first steps. When I looked at him now, music filled my head. The songs of our childhood, the songs of our future. It made me hopeful.

Today was my first day home. I had been keeping busy reading the first hardback copy of my sister's book, and she was home to help me get on and off the couch when I needed her. Macy came into the living room to answer the door, squeezing my shoulder on her way past the couch.

"Hey, Ter. You have a visitor," she said.

Gina sat next to me on the couch gently. I barely recognized her. Her hair was long and full, her skin was rosy, and she was grinning for the first time that I could remember.

"Gina! Thank you so much for coming over. I appreciated the emails while I was in the hospital. It sounds like you are doing much better."

She shook her head, "Well, I am still in a lot of counseling. But it is much better. I feel like I can finally breathe. And I have you and your sisters to thank for that."

Gina leaned forward and held my hand. Just like the first time, a jolt surged through my body. I gripped her hand as I saw the tile, shoes going over them in a hypnotizing rhythm.

Turning into the same room and Cathy lying in bed. I could see out of Cathy's eyes, her hurt and her loneliness. The same pillow going over her face. But this time, when her hands still, I see through her dead eyes as the pillow falls.

And it isn't Lucas on the other end. It's Gina, breathing hard and crying. I reeled back, snatching my hand away. Gina looked at me, confused.

"Are you okay?"

I forced myself to nod and looked down at her hands. The scratches were still red and angry. I looked back into Gina's face, her grin manic. I tried to put up psychic walls the way my mom had taught me, but Gina's frantic energy filled my mind.

Gina had been in a prison all her life, taking care of a mom who didn't know who she was anymore. Held captive by the man she thought she loved but who showed his devotion through bruises and empty promises.

Now, she only belonged to herself. She was finally free of her captors.

Nausea overtook me when I realized that the vision had come from Gina for a reason. I had been looking for the wrong killer all along. Gina was a monster; she had fooled me.

And I had helped her get away with it.

If you enjoyed meeting the Shaw Sisters in Sneakers in the Water, you won't want to miss the next chapter of their lives in the second installment of the Shaw Sisters Trilogy:

Stranger in the Shadows

Can true love survive death?

www.ingramcontent.com/pod-product-compliance
Lightning Source LLC
Chambersburg PA
CBHW032007170626
46807CB00006B/2691